Foreword

Deep in the Syrian desert, nestled between the dunes there lies a compound. Three acres of death hidden from God himself. Estimations on the number of men hired by the leader of this hell on earth lie in the hundreds. Every month a raiding party disembarks from the compound armed to the teeth and kills whole platoons worth of men. Decimating settlements and claiming weapons and bombs for themselves. This mindless violence and stockpiling of weapons has been going on without consequence for a myriad of years, no Government dares step in for fear of retaliation. For reasons known only to them, the Syrian government refused to step in and made it increasingly clear that if any other government attempted to step in it would be seen as an attempted invasion. With this in mind, no one even attempted to do anything; yet many people kept their eye on the Syrian Compound. When news leaked that the warlord in charge of the three acres of hell had purchased four tonnes of nuclear material the Governments paid a hell of a lot more attention to it. Yet they did nothing. However this complete and utter lack of effort from the governments that should be doing something sparked a mite of inspiration in one man: Thomas Stevens. A skinny, bespectacled tech millionaire of Asian descent. Ever since a young age Thomas 'please call' me Tom' Stevens had been obsessed with action Novels, reading them in-between investing classes. Now he was presented with an opportunity to live his secret wish: To be the leader of a tactical special operations team. To be an M to someone else's Bond. He finally had an excuse, a void had opened in the desert and no one else was choosing to close it. Thomas just had to find the right men and women to close it…

Introductions
"I am prepared to meet my maker. Whether my maker is prepared for the great ordeal of meeting me is another matter."

Chapter one: Hush

Scott Oliver sat behind the counter idly wiping his hands off onto his ragged apron. He waits, idly for the day to end so he can leave the butchers and enter the pub to slip into a regular malaise of alcoholism. Slowly pickling himself with beer after beer. The clock ticks by agonisingly. Second by Second, minute by minute. Only being interrupted by the entrance of a single customer who demanded twelve rashers of bacon, paid swiftly and left brashly. With the exeunt of this brief distraction Oliver glanced at the clock and realised only five minutes remained. With a smile and a stroke of his closely cropped hair that had begun to gray with age, he removed his apron. Stretching, he felt his muscles tense into iron beneath his shirt as he walked out of the shop door and into the frigid Nottingham air. He coolly released a humid lungful of air watching it turn into cloud in front of his eyes and begun his daily walk to his favourite watering hole: 'The spotted cock.' A crude name at worst and a poorly chosen one at best. The mascot of this unfortunately named was a rooster patterned with white spots and Scott always thought it would have been more aptly named 'The spotted rooster' or 'The roosting spotter.' He wasn't too bothered by it though, as he reasoned the pub wasn't his to name and he went there for the good beer not because of the name.

On the walk to the pub Scott found himself briefly believing that multiple people were following him and had to calm himself to stop his training forcing him to accost those that just happened to be going to the same pub. Now in the pub, Scott ordered his favourite: two pints of bitter. Ravenously, he practically inhaled the two pints and felt the steady haze of the beginnings of a drunken stupor begin to set in. He decided it was time to leave and climbed to his feet wearily keeping his eye on two young lads clad in black hoodies, who he was pretty sure had been watching him whilst they schemed in hushed voices. Sure enough as Scott headed to the door he heard the two lads rise, their stools squeaking on the wooden floor.

Letting the alcohol focus his mind, not cloud it he steadily walked out the door. Purposefully, he walked slowly so the boys could choose their fate. Simply walk away. Or follow him and learn what it meant to be in the SAS; retired but deadly nonetheless. Hoping to gain the upper hand he quickly skirted into a dark and uninviting alleyway and waited in the dank darkness for the boys to decide if they wanted to try their hands at becoming men. After a couple of unsettlingly quiet minutes the boys were around the corner and drawing knives menacingly. "Give us 'yer wallet" One of the boys squeaked, "yeah. Hand it over old timer or we'll have to stick you" the other squawked. "Lads, walk away. I'm giving you one chance here" Scott responded his gravelly voice growling in a low warning. The boys glanced at each other briefly clouded with doubt but it was clear they already made up their minds. "Give us your wallet"

"No I don't think I will, step away and I'll forget about it." The boys glanced in fear again before attempting to whisper amongst themselves, Scott caught glimpses of the conversation as he stood there muscles coiled, ready to pounce. *"Do you think we can take him?"*

"He's drunk, and remember he's loaded!" Scott thought back to the pub and inwardly cringed, when he'd opened his wallet to pay for the pints he had opened it all the way revealing his rather cushy SAS retirement pension. He chided himself mentally for this lapse; these lads probably wouldn't be doing this if they hadn't seen the wallet and now they were going to pay for his mistake. Accidentally he had tantalised them, baited them and they took it. With a start Scott flashed back to attention realising he'd been wrapped up in his own thoughts and the boys had finished talking. "How old are you lads? Do

you really want to do this over some petty cash?" For the first time Scott stared at the boys, they were practically identical. Both of them skinny Caucasian males of about sixteen draped in puffer jackets to make themselves look larger, one white, one black. A pathetic display, if Scott was honest with himself and it confounded him that these boys thought they could take him.

They were getting sick of waiting Scott could tell, the frustration and panic was beginning to build behind their eyes and it was only a matter of time before one of them tried something out of desperation. The silence curdled for a few endless seconds before finally the one in the black puffer jacket lunged brandishing the small knife like a lance. Scott stepped aside and grabbed the arm that wasn't holding anything as it sailed past him. The boys momentum had put him in a position where with his arm taut behind his back Scott could break his arm with the smallest movement. The boy in the white puffer jacket broke from his slack jawed surprise and rushed at Scott slashing wildly as he ran. Cursing Scott ducked and span the boy (who's arm he had held hostage) into his mate, still gripping the arm like a vice. Scott felt the boys in the black puffer jacket's bones crunch and slide agonisingly against each other as he wrenched the boy around. The spin put the boy with the broken arm right into the path of his friend who was still slashing rabidly as he charged. Scott winced as he heard the flailing blade slash the boy with the broken arm's torso open. That hadn't been his intention but he could make it work. Swiftly, he swung his feet around sweeping the legs of the boy before his friend could do any more inadvertent damage to him. He crashed to the ground with a sickening thump. Jumping to his feet Scott stared into the eyes of the bastard who cut his friend chin to hip by pure stupidity. "One last chance lad. Bugger off, or end up like your mate" Scott growled, his voice bloodied by exertion as he gestured to the moaning boy on the floor. The one still standing dropped his knife, presumably for fear of hurting his friend further and continued his feeble assault upon Scott. The boy charged at Scott, stubbornly refusing to learn from his mistakes and instead of dodging again like the boy expected him to Scott threw his arm with all the force he could muster placing all his weight into it and connected with the boy's face. Cartilage exploded in a geyser of blood as Scott's fist connected like a cannonball, definitely breaking his nose and quite possibly cracking his skull. The boy let out a short yelp before his eyes rolled into the back of his head and the ether claimed him sending him tumbling to the floor. Releasing a mighty sigh, Scott wiped some blood from his face and pulled his phone from his pocket to call an ambulance. Before he could even dial the second nine, the small sliver of light from the street outside which was lighting the alleyway disappeared. Glancing up in alarm Scott saw an SUV black as midnight blocking his escape. Two men armed with assault rifles disembarked menacingly and stared at him from behind the lenses of the aviators that seemed glued to their faces…

Chapter two: Bird

The London casino emanates sin. A large and seemingly endless floor-plan, Chintzy carpets and walls lined in gold. All scored by card's swish on velour, the slosh of drinks being poured, girls getting groped by their drunken boyfriends all out in the dim lighting of the Casino. Amelie sees and hears all this as she hurriedly walks to the bathroom. She clutches the duffel on her shoulder with a grip so tight her knuckles begin to whiten. After what she experiences as an eternity, she bursts through a door and into the dimly lit bathroom. To her relief she is alone and promptly Amelie locks herself in a stall. She still hears the rampant sin outside through the flimsy stall she's squatted in and smiles. No one would ever suspect her of what she was about to do and she knows it. Amelie: a slender girl with jet black hair, a hint of a French accent sneaking through her perfect English, and strikingly green eyes. She wasn't exactly the picture of crime but tonight she'd prove that stereotypes shouldn't be trusted. She giggled at the intoxicating thought and dumped her duffel bag on the floor. Amelie carefully drew the zip open and began the arduous task of assembling the book sized device in the bag. After many fiddly screws and bolts had been tightened and the three batteries connected, Amelie was ready…

She flicked the switch to power it on and smiled in subtle satisfaction as the drone's blades whirred to quiet life. Placing on the glasses she built specially to control the device, she instructed it to climb and watched as the sleek drone climbed in altitude to head height. She pressed the button labelled stealth on the frame of the glasses and watched in amazement as the drone turned completely invisible; only given away by a subtle tell-tale shimmer that could only be seen if you were at the right angle. Amelie laughed in delight before promptly clapping her hand over her mouth and glancing around anxiously as the sound reverberated. She had done it, her blood sweat, tears and engineering prowess had paid off. Watching from the perspective of the drone's camera through a small screen built into the lens of her glasses; she piloted the invisible quad-copter onto the game floor and situated it over the high-roller blackjack table. From her new angle she could see everyone's cards at all times and Amelie decided that she was ready.

Palming the wad of cash that lay rolled up in the duffel bag she walked confidently out of the stall and onto the game floor. She sweated as she handed the grand over to the dealer and dealt herself in. A grand was a lot of money to fork over to test a little engineering project of hers that had already cost a pretty penny to build.

The dealer handed Amelie her first card. She eyed up her opponent, a balding Asian man, and steeled herself. Hesitantly, she peeked at her first card. An ace, eleven off of the necessary twenty-one. Out the corner of her eye Amelie watched the Asian man's card from the perspective of her drone. He had a seven, he'd be insane not to draw, and sure enough in a thick American accent he demanded the dealer. "Hit me." Card slid across velour and the man slowly picked it up like it was a death sentence. An ace. A smirk slashed across the man's face before he silenced it with a blank expression. He now had eighteen and was content with his chances. "Hit me" Amelie said her voice cracking on "me" breaking into an unnatural falsetto. The faceless dealer slid another card over, unfazed by this strange display. Bending the card to grab a peek at the value Amelie mentally applauded herself, a ten. She now had twenty and her opponent only had eighteen. "I fold" the Man announced and Amelie echoed him, a dumb smirk spreading across her face as she resisted the urge to release a giddy laugh. Flipping his cards over so Amelie could see them the man sat cross armed with a cocky grin of his own. Sensing the danger in revealing her victory Amelie switched her expression to forlorn. The man spotted her expression and instantly fell for the bluff. "I'm sorry darlin' just reveal your cards and we can get this over with." He drawled. She did so and a grin exploded violently over her face as the man realised he'd been had. He stormed of grumbling angrily and Amelie claimed her chips from his side of the table.

Continuing like this Amelie managed to lose some, but win a lot more. Her pile of winnings increased in size exponentially until she'd accrued an amount in the neighbourhood of forty-eight thousand pounds. Amelie had just decided that she was going to keep going until fifty thousand when she felt a firmly threatening hand on her shoulder. Glancing at the owner of the hand she came face to face with an absurdly burly man in a suit so tight he appeared like he was about to pop; one of the casino's security guards. "I think it's best you come with me Ms." The security guard stated with a hint of ice in his voice. "What about my winnings?" Amelie stammered, her voice straying into a full blown French accent. "They'll still be here. It's best you comply Ms." The security guard's words were dangerous now and Amelie complied.

The security guard led Amelie out back of the casino and she looked around with dread building on the back of her neck. "Wait." The guard said staring off into a point in the middle distance. "For what?"

"Just wait."

A few awkward minutes passed before the backdoor opened and a man in a white suit and golden tie sauntered out. Amelie spotted the bulge of a gun in the lining of his jacket and gulped, she was getting a very bad feeling about all of this business. Staring at him with doe like eyes, she hoped he'd take pity on her and he'd let his guard down. "You've won too much I'm afraid 'luv. I can't let you keep fleecing my casino. Not to mention we found this in the bathroom" The suited man, presumably the owner, growled in a thick cockney accent slicking his greasy blonde hair back and tossing over Amelie's empty duffel bag. "We don't know how you did it but I think you cheated and whatever you did it with was in this bag" "I'm sorry sir, I didn't know I did anything wrong. I keep my makeup in that bag" Amelie cooed, purposefully letting her French accent take over and batting her eyelashes at him in a moment of quick thinking. Obviously taken aback he released the tension he was storing in his muscles and blinked, dumbfounded, for a couple of seconds. Then his face contorted into an ugly smile. "It's alright 'luv, how about you come back to my office and we forget about this." Disgusted, Amelie attempted to appease him. She walked up into his arms and let him paw at her as they walked back towards the door. As the pig leaned over to grab her rear his jacket parted and she saw the glint of cold steel, his gun. She lunged for it and successfully unhooked it from the pig's holster. Shaking like a leaf, she was now brandishing the man's pistol and the security guard hadn't noticed. He was still staring into the middle distance a hundred metres behind them.

The pig slowly raised his hands and looked at her, his eyes darting all over her face as he tried to determine how he had let himself be that gullible. "Careful now 'luv that guns got a hairtr-" Before the former owner of the London casino could finish his sentence Amelie's finger twitched, a symptom of her panic, and the gun trembling in Amelie's grip went off with a mighty bang. The shot tore right through the former owners forehead and all the life left his eyes instantly. His lifeless corpse threw itself towards the ground and connected to it with a muffled thump. In utter shock the gun tumbled from Amelie's shaking grip and followed the same path it's owner had seconds prior.

Amelie stood there for a good amount of time staring at the corpse and her own hands as her brain tried to comprehend what had just happened. What she had done. After an attempt at this processing she turned around and felt the cool kiss of a metal barrel on her forehead. The security guard had pulled himself out of whatever train of thought so ensnared him and he was now stood, his gun outstretched, pressing against Amelie, with an expression that of a dog owner who's dog has done something unspeakable on the carpet. "You killed my boss. Who's going to pay me now?" He said, peeved. "I don't know, I'm sorry. Please let me go." Amelie stammered, her girlish facade falling away and revealing her real self. "I've got to kill you so it looks like I did my job successfully" he said matter of factly. "No plea-" Amelie started but the man interrupted with a simple "Sorry" and a shrug. Clenching her eyes shut Amelie prepared for death. A gunshot reverberated around the concrete surrounding them and Amelie opened her eyes. There lying on the floor where he stood a moment before was the security guard.

In utter shock Amelie glanced around swiftly, attempting to determine the source of the sudden smiting. After a great deal of squinting, she spotted a man dressed in all black atop one of the nearby roof-tops. The man waved and gestured in-decipherability. She spent a few moments attempting to discern the meaning of the gestures before realising the man was in fact gesturing for Amelie to look behind her. She did so and came face to face with a skinny gentleman in a suit and sunglasses despite the fact that it was night and rather frigid…

Chapter three: Zeus

Hunting is an agonizing exercise in patience but Vladimir Stolenksy had mastered it. He could focus intently on one spot for hours without shifting, getting uncomfortable or being beckoned by his bladder. The man was a machine fine tuned for one thing, hunting. He could move silently into any position assemble his rifle in thirty seconds flat and kill you before you even knew he had the upper hand. Vladimir's father had taught him all this and given him the skills he needed to survive the life in the Siberian wilderness they both lead; as well as the skills necessary to survive during the Russian-Ukrainian war of 2022. Through his impeccable precision and talent with a rifle, Vladimir had ended up sniping for the Russian army racking up one-hundred and twelve casualties. After Russia's devastating loss, Vladimir decided that twelve years was long enough for a military career. Especially if those twelve years were as a decorated as they were for him.

Retired into freelance marksmanship for government, Vladimir spends his free time living out of a cabin in the Siberian stretch of forest that he grew up in. Any government that dared attempt to hire him would have to first dare to venture into the heart of frozen rejection to human life that was the Siberian forests. This didn't stop them however.

Whilst Vladimir waited to be activated, so to speak, he hunted animals and gathered firewood to survive. Even this he did meticulously, robotically, apathetically. Since he was a young boy Vladimir had been unable to feel empathy, only stating things as they were. Matter-of-factly. He sometimes wondered if this was a bad thing but then reasoned that if he wasn't wired this way he wouldn't be as effective as he was at hunting. Gradually, he became aware of his surroundings once more. The wad of snow he had been chewing to conceal his breath was now nothing but melt, yet he could see something frolicking in the dense wilderness.

A stag.

The sight reminded him of a memory from his childhood. A time when his apathy had reared its head and he had chosen practicality over emotion. Groggily, he shook the mental image away and zeroed in on the stag: it was a lean muscular work of art. Not much meat, but considering Vladimir was only one man it'd do just fine.

Plopping more snow in his mouth, something that had morphed into a habit that he supplemented with gum when he didn't have access to fresh snow, Vladimir adjusted his rifle and began to aim down the sights. Lining up the shot, he exhaled. Before he could squeeze the trigger and exalt the life from his glorious prey it darted to the left. Under his breath, Vladimir uttered damn in his native tongue. Picking up a handful of frost encrusted leaves, Vladimir crumbled them between his gloved fingers. They dashed apart into nothing and the wind carried them towards oblivion and where the deer happened to be standing. The wind had revealed his position. With a shake of his head Vladimir wearily climbed onto his feet and began the lengthy process of resettling where any prey wouldn't be able to catch an unfortunate whiff of him. Finally realigned, Vladimir began to wait again.

Within fifteen minutes the Stag showed it's horned head again and this time Vladimir had him. He squeezed the trigger and the stags eye exploded in a brilliant display of crimson. Straight through the eye and into the brain, best way to hunt an animal. Kills it instantaneously without ruining any off the meat. Now that great beast was felled Vladimir unhooked his gleaming hunting knife and stalked towards the stag. He was about to plant the blade in the rippled fur to begin the lengthy and messy process of skinning, taint the virginity of his gleaming blade with the holy sanctity of the hunt; when a hand rested itself firmly on the shoulder. Vladimir recognised the storied gesture from his military days and turned hesitantly around, lowering his gun in the process. Catching eyes with the culprit, A faceless goon in a suit, Vladimir nodded at him and the man explained "We have another job for you, come with me I'll take you to the chopper." Vladimir packed the deer into the snow, in an effort to preserve the hard earned meat, and clambered to his feet holstering the knife.

*   *   *

Stood on the roof-top of the building adjacent to the London Casino, Vladimir began disassembling the specialised rifle the Company that hired him gave him too use. Whatever it was Vladimir hadn't seen anything like it before, the company had told him it was a specialised prototype but it was assembled rather simply. Large clunky chunks of cutting edge technology held together by thumbscrews and tension slides. Now fully disassembled, Vladimir packed it into a bag and began the lengthy wait until he was debriefed. Wandering, his mind stumbled across his employer. Normally he was employed by governments but this time he was employed by an independent agency. On it's own it wouldn't be odd, but combined with this agency's seemingly infinite wealth and seemingly countless faceless suits Vladimir couldn't help but wonder who exactly he was dealing with. He couldn't care less about their intentions and who they hurt unless it was him they targeted. Yet, a gnawing curiosity began to creep in at the corners of his mind. The independent agency built this job up like it'd be the greatest of his career. However all he'd done so far is rescue an inept engineer. Creeping in was a feeling that this agency were going to have their way with him and he wouldn't be privy to why he was doing what he was unless absolutely necessary. Breaking him out his idle thoughts, one of the suits whistled at him in an antiquated code meaning 'oi what are you playing at?' Vladimir shot the suit a dirty glare and attempted to hand over the bag containing the prototype sniper. The suit shook his head and said "Mister Stolenksy, that gun belongs to you now. As long as you complete one more mission for us." The suit offered tonelessly. "I figured as much. What's the job?" Vladimir said in his precisely perfect English. "Can't tell you here, follow me" Vladimir obliged and began to follow the suit presumably to the independent agency's headquarters to be briefed on his mission...

Chapter four: Maple

Having grown up in Vancouver Canada, Many Americans looked down on Robin Anderson despite the fact she was ex-CIA and current FBI. In late 2023 these organisations had shifted from more investigatory branches of the government to pure Militia. Now in modern day America (2025) this shift was proving itself necessary; the population was beginning to tear at the seams. Bubbling over, the tension built to an intense crescendo before exploding in a brilliant salvo of violence. Men, Women and self styled hard-men (Gang betrothed teens) fought and stole in the streets. Devastatingly the entire country seemed to be lowering itself into oblivion, including the economy which was at the lowest it had been since the great depression.

Much like Germany in 1929, America was dancing on the edge of a Volcano and the people expected to control the mad masses were Robin and her cohort. Despite only being with the FBI for two years, she had swiftly inserted herself into the group and gained their trust even though she mostly ignored them. Robin wasn't bothered what they thought she was like as a person. All she wanted to do, desperately, was prove that she was just as good, if not better, than every burly grizzled in her strike team.

Today she would be given this chance. A disagreement between a petty thief and a security guard in the local mall had snowballed into a riot that was currently attempting to raze the aforementioned mall to the ground. The incensed group had begun destroying shops for the hell of it; Stealing food they desperately needed; Fighting like wolves and if the intel was to be believed had begun sleeping together in an orgiastic feral act of defiance. The insanity needed to be quelled before it spiralled more into depravity.

Robin sat swaying in the back of a SWAT truck clutching her hardened polymer riot shield and fingering the service weapon she had been ordered not to use unless absolutely necessary. Swaying with her, similarly clutching their own riot shields, were three other FBI agents. All three of them were older than Robin and more experienced, yet they all held mutual respect for each other in a reverence of sorts. They all sat silently anticipating the insanity they were about to be thrust shield forward into and they all accepted with solemnity that the mall's newfound inhabitants wouldn't take too kindly to the four of them. Clad head to toe in black armour plastered with the white letterhead of the Federal Bureau of Investigation, an institution that had become synonymous with riot control that wasn't exactly the gentlest, the inhabitants would immediately resist and quite possibly attack.

The van crunched to a halt on the asphalt of the Mall's car-park and everyone in the van began to count down from five in their heads waiting for the moment the doors would fly open. The doors flew open and everyone filed out clamouring to protect themselves with their shields. Towering over them, a monolith of aggression, the mall emanated foreboding. Faint screams could be heard and the flicker of flames licked the exterior of the building. Evaluating the inferno, Robin determined that it wasn't serious. The flames came from the dozens of electrical devices that had been haphazardly tossed out the windows of the mall and left to shatter into nothingness on the asphalt. Other than these discarded totems of consumerism, nothing else burnt and Robin nodded her approval at pushing forwards. Running across the car-park their shields made a heavy *clink clank* as they impacted against the armoured plates the group wore. Robin thought the noise resembled a war drum and smiled at the fear she knew they would instil in the smarter civilians.

They reached the entrance and realised the automatic doors' sensors were either broken or turned off. They didn't open and one of Robin's team members swung his battering ram into the glass repeatedly, keeping a weary eye on the brawling civilians that lay in the main foyer. Shattering in a deadly cascade of glass the door disintegrated, leaving nothing behind except the door's metallic frame. One by one, the shield carrying warriors filed through the vacant frame and faced the masses that lay in the foyer. Many of them had turned to face the group at the shattering of the glass, jaws agape. However a few of them remained locked in their brawls intent on beating their opponent, no matter what. At the top of her lungs Robin bellowed "Vacate the premises immediately or we will be forced to use violence!" Her riot helmet muffled her slightly as many people streamed out of the building, at first a trickle then an unstoppable current.

Once everyone who chose to leave had done so, the stubborn twenty or so remained, and for a moment silence prevailed. Then, as if god had fired a starting pistol, both the groups surged against each other simultaneously. The unstoppable force of the rioters meeting with the immovable object of the riot shields echoed in a violent clash that would reverberate through Robin's psyche for as long as she would remember. Fuelled by pure feral rage, the rioters clawed and shoved at the shields attempting to overpower them. Holding her shield with one hand, grinding her teeth against the strain, Robin unhooked a tear gas cannister from her hip and pulled the pin. Escaping in a continuos jet-like spew, the gas began to fill the foyer -and whilst the team was protected by the riot helmets- the crazed weren't and began coughing and spluttering, rubbing their eyes. It didn't stop the assault, only halted it momentarily. One leery man in particular, pushed defiantly against Robin's shield ignoring his teary eyes and tightening airways. His face was twisted into an in-human snarl and he was pushing robin back inch-meal. Unwilling to be bested, Robin took a swift step back sending the man stumbling forward as he no longer had Robin's shield to lean on. In the moment of his stumble she stepped forward again placing her momentum behind her shield and slamming it into the man. Reeling from the swiftness of the attack, the man's eyes rolled into the back of his head and he crumbled to the floor. With this development, the remainders in the foyer surrendered and with hands held high they filed outside peacefully and silently, where a police unit was waiting to arrest them. No doubt regretting their actions now that it was too late to change them. Taking a deep breath, Robin let the tension melt away from her shoulders. In theory that was the difficult bit done, now all that remained was to search each shop, nook, cranny and crevice and make sure everyone was gone or in handcuffs.

The group split up and Robin chose a clothing store that was situated to her left to begin her search. One by one she searched the aisles of bland clothing finding nothing except overpriced 'made in Taiwan' specials. Finally, she approached the curtained off lingerie section of the store and cautiously pushed the purple velvet aside. She could hear something strange. Heavy breathing and a noise resembling muffled screams echoed through the section and she beat a path towards the source of the bizarre noise, drawing her pistol. To Robin's great relief she only found a group of three men and seven women engaging in intercourse, half dressed in lingerie they pilfered from the now nude mannequins that circled them. Locked deep in the throes of passion the lewd collection hadn't noticed Robin. She fired a blank, jerking the lewd collection of criminals out of their gratification. Seeing an FBI agent in full black SWAT gear lugging a riot shield and holding a pistol, the lust driven civilians followed their smarter instincts and ran out of the shop trying, pointlessly, to claim some clothes to cover their unbridled shame. As if their dignity could be saved after that display.

Robin continued this way for some time, going from shop to shop clearing out lustful looters as well as lonely looters. To her relief Robin hadn't encountered any-more violent rioters since the foyer up to that point. Robin only had one more shop that she had to clear then she and the rest of the unit could leave, a job well done. Crossing the threshold Robin glanced to her left and her right, shield held in front of her. When she glanced to her right a fireball exploded across the surface of her shield and Robin stumbled back screaming a long string of profanities. Someone had decided it would be a good idea to chuck a Molotov cocktail at her. Presumably the unseen criminal had assembled it from the alcohol, rags and lighters the department store stocked. Steeling herself, Robin pushed forwards into the store again. This time the Molotov came from the left and she deflected it. "Fuck off!" A masculine voice screamed. "Surrender now, or I'll have no choice but to use lethal force!" Robin responded with her own Canadian tinted scream. The attacker didn't verbally respond, instead he answered by chucking another Molotov at Robin from the shadows. Deflecting it once more, Robin cut her hand on a piping hot shard of glass from the bottle. She waited till the burning alcohol had finished spidering its way across the shield then inspected her hand. It had been instantly cauterised by the flaming shard and wasn't particularly deep but it certainly irritated her. Staring into the shadows, she waited patiently and sure enough she saw the small flame of a lighter flicker to life. Quick as a shot Robin lowered the shield, held it horizontally and rested the arm holding her gun on top. Lining up the shot, she squeezed the trigger and watched the bullet ripped through the man just as he lit another Molotov. As he fell to the ground to die, the Molotov slipped out of his grip and shattered on the ground beneath him. His body came to rest in the flames and he screamed incessantly as he simultaneously barbecued and bled out. Staring blankly into the flames that were licking the cast iron cookware littering the shelves, Robin tuned out the screams. After blinking, hard, Robin finished clearing the store and sauntered out the way she came.

Regrouping with the rest of the unit in the parking lot she idly chattered, mentioning her encounter with the man in the department store. They all *oohed* and *ahhed* appropriately as she regaled her tale. After she was finished Robin noticed her colleagues focus fixed on a point behind her. She turned around and came face to face with a skinny suited man wearing a pair of dark sunglasses. Removing her riot helmet and holding it under her arm, Robin began to ask who he was when he interrupted. "We have a job for you Ms. Anderson, if you'd like to follow me…"

Chapter five: Nitro

Ivan Oleksiy had lived an incredibly rich military history, having served five years in the Ukrainian Army and three in Ukraine's special operations forces. Throughout his career he had used his charisma and immense friendliness to forge many rich and powerful friends. One of this illustrious group of friends was the one and only Thomas 'please call me Tom' Stevens.

On a holiday, Ivan was surprised to receive a summons from his old friend. Despite this confusion, Ivan still turned up to tend to his curiosity. The unlikely pair met in a small cafe to keep up appearances. As Ivan walked in he spotted Thomas and approached him with a haughty handshake. An odd sight they where indeed: a smiling grizzled Ukrainian fellow and a skinny sandy haired tech-millionaire.

Thomas began to explain, starting with: "Do you want anything to drink?"

"No thank you. It pleasure to meet you again!" An infectious grin spread across Ivan's face as he wondered what his old friend was up to. "I'm sure you're wondering why after so long I called you?"

"Yes, explanation would be appreciated." Ivan stated, his smile breaking into his voice. Unfortunately, before Thomas could delve further into the subject; a waiter approached and ask the pair what they would like to order. Waving the waiter off and gesturing to indicate a lack of interest Thomas turned his attention back to Ivan's weather-beaten yet joyous expression. "Ivan, as I'm sure you know for a while now a lot of problems have been cropping up that many governments have been unwilling or unprepared to deal with." Thomas said, a hint of weariness creeping in as well as a mighty sigh. "Course I know. It all over news." Ivan responded in his broken yet endearing English. "Yeah, well I want to fix that. I'm going to assemble a

team and fix these issues for the government." Ivan thought for a couple of seconds in wonderment. "That work, I suppose."
"Are you in then my friend?"
"In? Me?"
"Yes old friend, I want you on my strike force."
"Yes course I in, why not I be?" Ivan said laughing. Shaking hands, the two smiled at each other and Ivan fetched them both a coffee from the previously dismissed waiter. The two friends talked for a long while, enjoying each-others newly rekindled friendship. Ivan's infectious charisma wormed it's way into Thomas and he loosened, forgetting about the cramps that were his companies and assets. Carrying on this way for an hour that quickly spiralled into two, the two old friends caught up. Fully caught up with each other Thomas' voice strayed into his businessman tone once more. "Back on topic, I have something I think you'll like old friend." Ivan raised his eyebrows but said nothing in response.
Following Thomas he stayed silent, jovially wondering what surprise lay in store for him now. To his astonishment, Thomas took him to a helicopter atop a building down the street from the cafe. Once the two where secured inside the lavish helicopter, it began the take off procedure. With a kicking whir the propeller began to spin completing hundreds of revolutions a second. Throughout the journey Ivan stared out of the window, wonder slacking his jaw.
After a lengthy journey, the helicopter landed in a picturesque landscape. They where surrounded by rolling green hills and all forms of isolated nature. Ivan knew better than to ask where they were. Thomas began walking off towards the hills suddenly and Ivan had to jog to catch up. "Beautiful place" muttered Ivan, still accented by his eternal smile. Surprising Ivan, Thomas responded to the barely audible train of thought. "You get used to it unfortunately." Surprised by his old friends

newfound cynicism, Ivan didn't respond and instead kept walking in silence with a grin plastered to his weary face.

An hour and a half later the pair arrived at what appeared to be a dilapidated hangar nestled between two grassy knolls. Thomas stopped and gestured for Ivan to enter. With his Smile dampening to a smirk, Ivan pushed open the creaky door and was astonished to find not an old hangar but instead a state of the art testing range. He faced a shooting range with moving targets; a small assault course and (strangest of all) a selection of brick walls. Walking in behind him, Thomas entered with a smile and outstretched arms. "It's wonderful isn't it? And this is our cheap one!" Thomas span around, arms outstretched as if he was trying to ascertain the very essence of the place. Cocking his head Ivan asked "All this? And there more? Why?" In response Thomas let out a haughty laugh that echoed through the space wonderfully and pleased Ivan. Walking over to a weapons locker that was inlaid in the wall, Thomas opened it and pulled out something that had the appearance of a black yoga mat. He handed the black mat to Ivan with an incredible smile and Ivan was surprised at how deceptively heavy it was. Thomas took it out of Ivan's hands and unfurled it, plastering it onto one of the random walls on the shooting range. Once this was achieved, Thomas sauntered back over to Ivan and palmed off a small charging plunger. Staring at the yoga mat-like device, Ivan determined it must be some sort of breaching charge. Copper wire ran the edges of the pad and in the centre there was a small black box. Glancing at Thomas for confirmation, Ivan removed the safety cover and pressed the plunger down.

On this action the copper wire burst into brilliant flame cutting through the wall cleanly. Right before the flame met itself once more a mechanical *clunk clunk* was emitted by the box and the other side of the wall lit up as if a bomb had been detonated back there. With this done the burned chunk of wall fell away leaving a hole large enough for a man to climb through with ease. Catching sight of Ivan's expression of awe, Thomas exclaimed: "Magnesium!" Whilst clapping his hands together and throwing his head back, barking another laugh. "It creates the effect of a flash-bang for anyone on the other side, disorienting them. It's excellent isn't it?" Ivan's grin returned as understanding dawned on him. "It's incredible."

"I'm glad you think so, it's yours." Ivan stood dumbstruck once more before gathering his wits and responding, "Mine?"

"All yours to use in any mission, all you got to do is help me with my mission. So one last time, are you in?" Thomas held his hand out and Ivan took it, clasping Thomas' tiny yet strong grip in his bear-claw. With a nod the two were ready…

Operator Files
"Everyone always says 'know thy enemy'. Knowing thy allies
is a lot more important for survival. Teamwork is everything"

*All of these are written by Thomas, a
licenced psychologist and the engineering crew.*

Operator File One

"A six inch blade never needs to be reloaded"

Real Name: Scott Oliver
Call-sign: Hush
Speciality: Stealth and speed
Date and Location of Birth: 25/11/1985 Nottingham, England
Experience: 13 years in the SAS, Multiple records for speed in SAS kill houses
Physch Evaluation: Scott holds a high value on stealth and efficiency. Claiming that he believes Electrics are too much of a crutch for modern day soldiers. He expounds saying that modern operators spend too much time watching cameras and trying to determine where the enemy are instead of just entering the building and relying on your training and talent to determine where the Tango's are. Pulling out a small switch blade, Scott explains how a blade will never let you down and how one of his biggest pet peeves is when operators, as he puts it, "fanny about too much and don't just get in the bloody building, They should just get in there and plant a blade in the Tango's necks." He then explains his view on teamwork. "When every operator works like a cog in a well oiled machine I will get on well with 'em. But if they don't understand their place and what's actually important in the operation we'll have issues." Retired for seven years from the SAS, you'd think Scott had begun to get rusty but the exact opposite is true. He honed his skills further whilst working as a butcher in retirement and is as swift and efficient as ever. In my professional opinion, he will be a very efficient operator that will push the rest of the team to work their hardest. However, if he feels a member of the team isn't pulling their weight he might cause an issue or altercation. Proceed with caution with him.

Operator Notes: When Hush was asked what he wanted he said stealth. So we've given him a silenced browning high-power pistol as a subtle reminder to his storied career in the SAS. We've also given him a gold plated aluminium hunting knife with gold filigree inlaid into the cherry wood handle. Furthermore to complete his efficiency and stealth trifecta, we've provided him with a selection of smoke grenades and flash bangs so he can disorient the enemy before introducing them to his blade.

Operator File Two

"Information is everything, and I'm the eye in the sky"

Real Name: Amelie Monet
Call-sign: Bird
Speciality: Tech, Cameras and reconnaissance
Date and location of birth: 06/09/2003 Champagne, France
Experience: none
Physch Evaluation: Despite living in France until the age of fourteen, Amelie speaks perfect English; her French twang only comes out when stricken by intense emotion. She talks to me in a very professional and even tone, slipping to a childlike wonder as she explains how she found her love for engineering. Amelie tells me about her move to England and how she would stare at the car manufacturing plant that was across the street from her and wonder how they made them. Slipping into the giddy, she tells me about her first car. Which she tuned by hand. When asked about how she did this, Amelie just says that she took it apart and then put it back together, but better. Amelie begins to tell me about her true passion: Cameras and photography and her giddiness practically radiates off her. "As soon as the money for my car left my bank account I was saving for a camera. As soon as I got my paws on it I tried to figure out how to make it portable so I could take photos from anywhere." Amelie Monet is an incredibly mechanically minded and tactical operator. However I fear that with her lack of combat experience she won't cope well with the stress of active combat, she will be effective in the team, I just can't professionally suggest she goes into combat.
Operator Notes: Not much is known about Bird's Wing drones. From the small amount of time we've had with one of them, they are standard basic small quad-copter style drones with a miniaturised 360 degree camera mounted on the bottom.

Furthermore, they can go practically invisible by refracting the light around them to blend perfectly into the environment. Powered by three LiPo 11 volt racing batteries, The drones can continuously operate for three hours without the invisibility engaged and one with it it engaged. This light, low power solution also allows them to fly with such a low revolution rate on the propellers that the drone remains in the air barely audible.

<u>Operator File Three</u>

"I am an artist, and the wall behind my target is my canvas"

Real Name: Vladimir Stolenksy
Call-sign: Zeus
Speciality: Marksman
Date and location of birth: 19/11/1989 Somewhere in the Siberian wilderness, Russia
Experience: 12 years in the Russian ground forces as a marksman
Physch Evaluation: Vladimir stares intensely at my face as if trying to discern the best place to plant a bullet. Through the interview he remains withdrawn. Barely answering some of my questions and outright refusing to answer others, he moves with the practised grace of a hunter and speaks slowly. precisely. Every word he rolls around his mouth as if deciding exactly what he wants to say. Vladimir admits he gained his marksmanship experience in the Russian-Ukrainian war of 2022 but doesn't explain further than that. His file states he caused 112 casualties but he seems surprised by that number, instead deflecting to his childhood where he was raised by his father. He explains that he and his Father lived in a shack in the Siberian forest hunting for animals for food. When I probed further about his Father he began telling me about a deer he befriended as a child "Her name Was Alisa. She was a beautiful doe, innocent. Careless. I would see her sometimes in the woods. I told my father about her and he made me tie a bow to her so I would always know which deer she was. A beautiful pink bow. Then winter came. It was one of those dangerous winters for my father and I. We ran out of heat and we ran out of food. Then on one of our desperate hunting trips I saw Alisa. Me and my father ate well that night and I learned compassion was the enemy of survival." After this admittance I ended our

meeting. However in my professional opinion, Vladimir will be an excellent operator and will follow any order issued to him. However his reclusivity may become a problem when he's forced to work with other operators.

Operator Notes: For Zeus we spent ten million dollars designing the lightning-mk01. We plan to unveil this rifle at the world weapons convention next year in 2026. The Zeus rifle is the first 50. BMG class rifle to have zero recoil. This is achieved by 12 separate gas vents drilled into the barrel, allowing the explosive gas to dissipate without slowing the velocity of the bullet. The lightning-mk01 also has a rotating drum magazine that has six different compartments that allows the user to switch ammunition from a selection of: standard BMG, tracers, explosive ordinance, incendiary, tranquillizer and hollow-point. The scope in itself is a work of art. It has an adjustable magnification. It can go from 1x all the way to 500x, an arguably unnecessary range. Furthermore, the scope has a further two optional settings: A thermal infrared camera to see targets through brick walls and a patented big-brother tech scanner. This scanner allows the scope to see electrical devices through walls; allowing the operator to locate and eliminate hidden traps such as grenade tripwires and IED's.

Operator File Four

"A good defence is the best offence"

Real Name: Robin Anderson
Call-sign: Maple
Speciality: Shield operator
Date and Location of Birth: 29/02/2000 Vancouver, Canada
Experience: 2 years in the CIA, 4 years in the FBI
Physch Evaluation: Robin is eager to prove she's worth her salt, so to speak. In our interview she introduces herself with a firm handshake and a piercing gaze into my eyes. I enquire about what made Robin want to join the special forces and she begins to tell me about the ice hockey teams in Vancouver. "As long as you were okay with taking a puck to the face you could join no matter your gender. Different story for you yanks though. When I moved to America I looked for a new hockey team; I had to join an all female one. I wasn't allowed to play with the men and prove myself. Since then I wanted to get to the highest branch of the US and prove that I can do it as a woman amongst men." From there we continued to talk about her beliefs. In my professional opinion, she will be effective in the team. However, she has a tendency to doubt herself and if she believes the men of her team are better than her she will strive until she is at her limit. She might need continued support from a counsellor as her strong strive to be as good as others is a front to hide the insecurity that she believes she isn't good as others.
Operator Notes: For Maple we constructed a polymer, bullet proof, riot shield. Due to its sling strap design it can be operated with one hand whilst the operator fires with the other hand. The shield can instantaneously freeze the front face of it using two water jets mounted to the front and a dry ice compartment. The water jets can be operated independently of

the dry ice, not to freeze the shield but instead to stop Tangos in their tracks. Then by turning on the dry ice, Maple can freeze the water that is soaked into the enemy's clothes. Slowing them down and inhibiting their thoughts by the sudden onset of hypothermia. If the shield freezes it's front face it provides a protective sheen that protects the operator using it from the blinding light of flash-bangs. It can also provide an extra layer of protection against a flame thrower and other flame weapons as the shield will remain at 0 degrees until the ice is entirely melted.

Operator File Five

"demolition is mercy"

Real Name: Ivan Oleksiy
Call-sign: Nitro
Speciality: Demolition and team leader
Date and location of birth: 03/04/1996 Kiev, Ukraine
Experience: 5 years in the Ukrainian army, 3 years in
Ukraine's Special Operation Forces
Physch Evaluation: Ivan, despite the macabre nature of his
work is incredibly jovial. He is upbeat and almost puppy-like
in his mannerisms. He is incredibly friendly, however after
reviewing his training tapes I can't help but wonder if this
jovial attitude is a front so people around him drop their
guards. After our introductions he got around to describing how
he got into the world of secret services: He explained how
fighting in the Russian-Ukrainian war of 2022 changed him
from a pessimist to an eternal optimist. "Men no survive with
not good outlooks, I learn how to have good outlook" He says
in somewhat broken English; whilst absent-mindedly fiddling
with the arms of the chair. Ivan then explained the value he
holds dearly on team work, saying if it wasn't for the excellent
teamwork the Ukrainian army displayed (and joking if it wasn't
for the terrible teamwork of the Russian army) then they
wouldn't have won. In my professional opinion, Ivan will be
incredibly useful for the team, being able to mediate the other
the other operators in the group. However, it remains to be seen
how he will interact with a Russian operator.
Operator notes: For Nitro we personally engineered a sticky
polymer pad that will stick to virtually any material. Attached
to the pad is a 1 lb block of C4 mixed with magnesium. The
magnesium will ignite with the remote detonation of the C4.
Anyone unlucky enough to be on the receiving end of the wall

charge will be temporarily blinded. This gives the operators in tow time to enter the building through the newly created hole and situate themselves with the upper hand whilst the opposition is blinded.

Training

"I hated every minute of training, but I said, 'Don't quit. Suffer now and live the rest of your life as a champion.'"

Chapter One

Hush stared at the people surrounding him, trying to read who they were off their faces. He didn't know how he felt about the call-sign's they had all been assigned. To him they were dreadfully childish, however many of the operators on the team didn't share this view. Bird, a young French girl who Hush had heard hadn't had combat experience, loved hers. She exclaimed in delight when she saw the rest of the operators and in a French coloured accent had asked everyone their call-sign. Nitro, a friendly Ukrainian and the team lead, had quickly asserted himself with a firm handshake and a massive grin for everyone. Even the Russian sniper got a handshake and a smile, much to his chagrin. Maple, the Canadian shield operator stayed in a corner scowling at everyone and much like Hush, was attempting to determine everyone's past. A lull fell over the groups quiet chatter and Nitro took his opportunity. He climbed to his feet, a friendly mountain amongst frigid icebergs and began to address the room at large. "Hello all! You must be confused to why we have been assembled-" Everyone shared a quick glance before turning their attention back to nitro. "-I assure it a necessary cause. At current time I can't tell you where exactly we be deployed-" A knowing smirk shot across Zeus's face as his eyebrows shot up. His face turned back into marble before anyone else could notice. "-We just need train to be best there is. You all been given a specialised gadget. Today we familiar ourselves with them. We practice in a mock up of the Iranian embassy." Now it was Hush's turn to grin. "Do you have something to say, Hush?" Nitro turning his blazing amusement onto Hush and Hush responded. "Surely I 'av an upper hand 'ere. Every two months I ran through a mock-up of the Iranian embassy with the SAS." Nitro laughed and clapped a hand on Hush's back. "That why we made alterations, I'm sure you have fun. Now wait we be sent through soon." Nitro sat back down and dwarfed the cheap plastic construction of his fold-out chair. Now in silence, the five operators continued staring at each other. The only one who wasn't engaging in this strange ritual was Zeus; who instead sat confidently inspecting his newfound limb. Every other operator understood each others gadget, but Zeus's remained a mystery; despite Hush and Nitro both independently asking Thomas about it. The strange rifle was locked behind a veil of top secret, yet Zeus already moved with it as if it was an extension of his very body.

As Zeus cleaned and partially dismantled his rifle, Hush stared intently at it trying to determine what brand of new age bullshit it was. Everyone else stared around the facility they were sat in. A warehouse constructed from corrugated iron and concrete located somewhere deep in the Scottish Highlands, it strikingly resembled the hangars of the SAS's Hereford base. This fact put Hush more at ease than he should have been. The only person that knew the truth was Nitro, beyond the hangar door accented with a large reed industrial light lay one of the most high tech facility's in the world. Behind that barrier was two-hundred square feet of alloy and polymers, lit by LED's galore. Having overseen its construction, Nitro was still in awe. The facility looked like it wouldn't be out of place on a space station two hundred years in the future. This would be the true test though, was the team good enough to beat the first stage of their training?

Bird sat in her chair, resisting the urge to frantically glance around. Even though she wouldn't admit it to a soul, she was terrified. Never been in combat, never seen any action, she was sweating bullets at the prospect of entering what was colloquially known as a 'kill house'. The sight of the other female operator looking confident didn't help either, Maple was calm, composed and ready to prove herself, clutching her heavily modified shield whilst smirking. Whilst Bird was the complete opposite. As she pretended to recline in the chair comfortably, her anxiety's ran wild. Like A rabid dog in a butchers shop. She had never done anything like this before, would she be a savant or flop on her face? Bird was pretty sure it would be the latter. As she kept running these thoughts over her mind, like rough cloth over a loom, the industrial work-lamp clicked over from a deep red into an alluring green. Well hidden speakers crackled to life with an electrical whine and all the operators glanced upwards towards the source of the dreadful racket. Thomas's voice came over the speakers, the voice of God, heavily sullied by cheap electricals. "In two minutes those doors will open, your job is to clear the entire premises. You and the hostiles are all equipped with flour rounds, this training exercise is incredibly safe." Everyone except Bird ejected their magazines and inspected them. Sure enough they were all marked with a white stripe indicating non-lethal flour would be the only ordinance these bullets delivered. Perfect for a training exercise as any operator that failed would be clearly marked with a white smear of shame. "The following exercise is a mock-up of the Iranian embassy siege. The exterior of the building is exactly the same, however the floor-plan is completely changed in order to avoid giving some groups an unfair advantage." Hush's facial expression flashed into a moment of uncertainty before his face melted back into cockiness once more. "Here's your briefing operators: according to our intel there is approximately twelve hostiles in the building." A low whistle escaped Hush's lips. "Damn, double the original embassy siege."

"Same amount of operators though." Bird stammered quietly, attempting to hide her worry. "Anyway team, they have seven hostages and have many grenades. However, since they entered the grenades haven't been seen again. We can only assume they were used in the construction of booby traps. Rely on teamwork, use your gadgets and good luck." The incessant speaker whine cut out and another cacophony replaced it.

Grinding metal echoed throughout the warehouse as every operator climbed to their feet and turned on their earpieces. Now was the time, they would work together for the first time and truly experience each others flaws in combat. Imposingly, the doors slid open and revealed The Embassy...

Chapter Two

The embassy was a perfect replication with some alterations to the décor, Instead of white marble and concrete it was black marble accented with blue LED's. This modernism gave the effect that it wasn't a replication of the kings row Iranian embassy in a top secret warehouse, but instead was a grand vision of a future space colony. Instead of a sky they were surrounded by the void as a black dome surrounded them and the building. After a moment of standing there dumbfounded the group surged on forwards towards the building. Lagging slightly behind, Bird swallowed hard and nervously gripped the bag containing her drone. Even since the great success at the casino, she still had some worries about her drone and Bird couldn't help but feel the same anxieties she had that night in the casino. Grip tightening and knuckles whitening once more, she gripped the bag ever harder and fell back into step with the rest of the group.

Zeus began to swerve away from the group heading to the left of the building. Nitro turned a questioning eye onto him and in response Zeus raised a hand and pointed a previously unseen watchtower to the side of the Embassy. "Hunting nest."

"Happy hunting." Hush muttered as he forged his way ahead to the Embassy. "I say we detonate a distraction charge on the roof's skylight-" Hush declared nodding to Nitro "-Then I say, two of us repel up the back and go through the skylight, the other two go through the front door."

"Sorry, but isn't that exactly what the SAS did with the embassy Siege?" Maple questioned in her lyrical Canadian accent. "Not exactly, but it's close enough to work."

"Sorry, but surely Thomas will be expecting that? We need to think of a different plan entirely." Maple continued. "Sorry Hush. She right." Nitro said. Hush kept quiet and gestured for the pair to continue as a surly expression fell across his gas-masked face. "We detonate distraction charge." Nitro said.

"Then send in Bird and Hush through the skylight. Bird can flush them out with her drone and then Hush can quietly deal with them." Bird frantically nodded in response and Nitro continued: "Other two push front entrance. With luck they be guarding window upstairs, Zeus take care of them and we be safe."

"With a bit of luck we should clear them out and be home in time for tea then?" Hush said, voice clearly jaded by cynicism. "I guess so, it makes sense to me." Bird said quietly. "What? Speak up I can't 'ear you." Hush shouted obtusely. "She said, it makes sense to her. Sorry if you can't understand." Maple said lurching out from behind her heavy shield and standing up for Bird. "Okay then, whatever." Hush said; surliness overtaking him once more, like a teenage boy told he can't go out with his friends.

Hush and Bird firmly secured their ropes to the edge of the modern monolith and began to repel up it, climbing up it horizontally as if they were walking up the building itself. Glancing down at the astro-turf masquerading as the perfectly manicured back garden of the Embassy, Bird had to resist the overwhelming urge to gag. Hush noticed her discomfort with the height and rolled his eyes to himself. This woman had a lot to learn. Reaching the roof, the unlikely duo unhooked their ropes and began to crouch their way to the central skylight. Peeking hesitantly over the edge, the pair saw a lone guard stood alone in a room. Carefully, Bird assembled her drone and began to pilot it onto the skylight. Using the propellers she began to cut a small X onto the centre of the panel. This panel would allow Hush to drop down and break the glass, not quite the waste of resources a thermal charge would be but close enough. With the X complete Bird flew the drone away from the skylight and back into her palm. Touching his ear and activating the earpiece, Hush announced to the group:

"Operation Smite is a go." Before Bird could give him the thumbs up Hush jumped at the glass panel, drawing his knife. The hostile in the room glanced up as a shadow fell over him and the last thing he saw was Hush falling on top of him. Hush mimed slitting his throat and the Hostile declared "Out" before pretending to be dead. One down, eleven to go. Climbing to his feet, Hush looked up to watch Bird slowly fumbling her way down the skylight. Shaking his head, he placed his finger over his ear again as the small shell buzzed to life. "Operation painfully obvious is a go." Maple said over the earpiece…

As Hush and Bird were entering from the roof Nitro and Maple convened at the entrance, patiently waiting for Zeus to strike any Hostile that revealed his unfortunate self. The silence was interrupted by two shots. Starting in alarm, the two glanced up and saw flour blooming against the windows. It seemed the God of lightning had done his job and struck with his lightning bolt. Three down, nine to go. The silence barely had time to settle again before the distinct sound of shattering glass echoed throughout the dome. Sharing a smile, the two flung the doors open as Maple announced over the earpiece; "Operation painfully obvious is a go."

Maple pushed forwards with her shield held tightly to her chest. A bud of flour spattered itself across her shield and she turned to the source of the annoyance. Coming face to face with a Hostile she turned on the water jets and dowsed him. Nitro used the moment of disorientation and planted a shot of flour between his eyes. The flour mixed with the water and seeped into his eye, stinging and burning. "Ow! Fuck man. Out." The Hostile said falling to the ground and pretending to be dead as he ferociously rubbed his eyes, attempting to remove the concoction. Four down eight to go.

The man on the floor was the only Hostile in the room, presumably the rest would be on the second or third floor.

Glancing around for a door to somewhere else in the building, the pair noticed a door tucked off to the side. Maple tried it and upon discovering it was locked, drew her shield back to smash the door off of it's hinges. Nitro planted his hand on her shoulder, before she could though. At the shake of his head and giant smile she acquiesced. "I have better idea." He said, confidently, his grin somehow growing even more. Pulling out a charge from his bag, Nitro began to knock along the wall looking for where there was something on the other side. Eventually his knock rang hollow and he unfurled the pad. Sticking the pad to the wall, he gestured for Maple to stand back. With the gleaming black charge planted on the wall, Nitro ran behind Maple and her shield and pressed the detonator's plunger firmly down. Cleanly and efficiently, the wall was sliced like butter. A split second before the hunk fell to the floor a *fwomp fwomp fwomp* echoed as the charge released flash-bangs. The newly created entrance then exploded in a brilliant blaze of glory, blinding the Hostiles on the other side. Three stood around a conference table in there; hands over their eyes shouting incomprehensible orders to each other. Working together, two cogs of a well oiled machine, Maple soaked them and Nitro shot them. "out." Echoed thrice as they were taken out one by one. Seven down, five to go. Once the pair were confident that the room was clear they began to approach the door directly opposite the newly created one they had entered through. Throwing it open, the pair came face to face with a bomb in the neighbouring conference room. Maple grabbed her eyepiece and shouted into it. "There is a bomb I repeat there is a bomb, diffusion necessary."
Hushes voice echoed back over the earpiece. "Fuck! Okay how long have we got?" Bird squinted round the corner at the large suitcase full of wires and packages and searched it with her eyes. After a couple of moments she found it, a small red timer clicking down. "We've got five minutes." An audible sigh was

heard over the earpiece before being followed by a single forlorn "Aye."

With their intel shared, Nitro clapped Maple on the shoulder to proceed. She did so and as soon as she crossed the doorways threshold she tripped on something and fell to the ground as an ear-splitting bang reverberated around the conference rooms. Desperately, she looked down and saw Nitro also on the floor at her feet. Seconds later, she realised that regrettably the pair are covered head to toe in flour. Maple tried to determine the source of the flour and noticed a small grenade on one side of her, and the pin and string on the other. A booby trap, she was out and so was Nitro because she hadn't looked at her feet despite being explicitly told to. She and Nitro both uttered "Out" in unison and glowered at the Hostiles that had tucked themselves out of sight, hoping the pair would be so distracted by the bomb they would walk aimlessly through the door.

Back on the third floor, Hush was pacing. Taking measured step after measured step. He and Bird had cleared the third floor fully together and escorted all seven hostages out a window. Along the way they had dismantled many grenade tripwires, Hush spotting them moments before Bird had blundered into them on many occasions. Together they had just barely taken out three terrorists. Not including the one they killed on entry. Hush had silently taken down two and Bird had blundered into the third. She placed a flour bullet between the man's ribs and wouldn't stop apologising to him as he pretended to be dead. Ten down and two to go, Hush was beginning to worry. "Bird, We all have diffuser kits right?"
"Yeah- It's standard equipment, I think." Bird stammered, still reeling from the over-stimulation of the training exercise.
"Yeah I thought so, I think our boys have gotten into a spot of trouble. Probably a grenade tripwire."

"Maple's shield is big and clunky so she might not of noticed the wire, I didn't and I don't have a shield obscuring my view." Bird practically whispered. "Damn it. Good point. Bloody shield operators. I say we push down the stairs and take the bomb site. They're can't be too many Tangos down there." Maple held a hand out and pulled her drone out once more. "What's that gonna' do?"

"Give us intel." Bird began to pilot the drone through the building, slipping through half open doors and eventually down the stairs. "Come on. We've got to move it there's only three minutes left." Bird ignored Hush's rising annoyance and kept focusing on piloting her drone. She looked through the ever infinite maze of corridors until she came along a row of conference rooms all interconnected. Entering the first with her drone Bird spotted a rectangular hole in the wall leading to the lobby. "Nitro." She muttered under her breath. Hush glanced at his watch pointedly and said "Two minutes."

"Give me a moment!" Bird shouted desperately. Taken aback by this sudden shift in volume, Hush said nothing but resolved to do it his way. He rushed out the room, bounded down the stairs and headed the direction he saw the drone head in Bird's glasses screen. Eventually, he reached the first conference room and stared at the door to the next one. It was pulled shut but he could see flour accenting the bottom of it. This door had recently seen some action, and not in the good way. Whatever that may be for a door. Swiftly kicking into action, Hush planted his boot on the centre of the door sending it flying open with a *crash*. On the floor lay Nitro and Maple pretending to be dead, and stood over them were two Hostiles.

Making eye contact with one of them, Hush dropped to one knee and shot them both before they could draw their weapons. Twelve down, none to go. Scott grinned, a rare grin no one but the men he killed saw, and pulled the diffuser out of his pack.

Before he could even open it a large explosion echoed over hidden speakers and Hush cursed...

Chapter Three

All five of them stood in a small shed like structure in which was situated a heavy wooden desk. Behind this desk was Thomas, who was a bizarre mix between frustrated and amused as the group attempted to ascertain what would happen next. The only one that hadn't failed their part of the mission, in theory, was Zeus. Yet he still was stood lined up at ease with them, ready to accept a reprimand. Thomas's expression was that of subtle disappointment and his lengthy sigh accented his point rather well. "Five of the worlds best operators couldn't diffuse a bomb." He said weightily. "Sorry sir, but we all did the mission exactly as you told us to. You didn't tell us it would be a bomb diffusing situation, it's not our fault." Maple defiantly spoke up. For a moment no one said anything, then Thomas climbed to his feet and drew himself to his full, not very imposing, height.

"Zeus, may I have a look at your rifle?" The savage Russian veteran nodded, pulled his rifle from his shoulder and held it out, an arcane offering to his suited God. The suited God of the team took the gun and struggled to maintain his grip on the heavy rifle. "See this Zeus?" he said gesturing to an extra dial on a scope. "You can change it to Electro Magnetic sensing mode. This allows it to-"

"See electronics through walls." Zeus interrupted, disappointed in his own lapse of judgement. "Including-"

"Bombs." Zeus finished off Thomas's sentence and hung his head low. Despite being an excellent hunter he had forgotten rule number one: know thy enemy. "Zeus, you were too focused on the windows. Yes you took two Hostiles down, but after that point you should have gathered intelligence. Located traps, bombs and heat signatures. Instead all you did was stare at the same windows. You aren't hunting stupid animals without complex thought. You are hunting humans. One or two die near a window they are going to be smart enough to not go near windows again. You wasted your time." Thomas tutted and handed the heavy rifle back over. "I didn't have time to familiarise myself with the Rifle's ability's sir." Zeus said, re-shouldering the hunk of futuristic death. "No you didn't, granted, however you did read the engineer's report on it. You didn't even try to do anything other than basic marksmanship. I might as well take that off you and give you a Kar98K." Thomas said gesturing to the rifle resting on Zeus's shoulder. "Learn to use it and all its abilities or fuck off, you got that?" Mildly surprised by the sudden outburst, Zeus said nothing as Thomas took his seat back behind his plush desk and turned his attention to Maple.

"What? I'm sorry but I did nothing wrong? I couldn't see the wire because of my shield." She said, ever defiant. "You utilised your equipment perfectly Maple." Thomas said with a smile that could give Nitro's usual some competition. The smile vanished as quickly as it appeared and he continued. "However, you seem to have somewhat of an attitude when addressing me."

"What do you mean?" Maple said the ice in her voice chillier than ever. "I think you meant to say, what do you mean, Sir or what do you mean Tom." Thomas said as Maple fought against the irresistible urge to roll her eyes. "Improve this or you'll be removed from this team. The trap wasn't your fault, I understand that. You need your team to spot them for you and today they let you down." Thomas turned his attention onto Hush. "Hush, you expertly worked with stealth. You took down three Hostiles without alerting any others. However, you actively refused to work properly with Bird. Yes you helped her dismantle door traps but you barely talked to her. She doesn't have training, you need to teach her not treat her like a child."

"Wait sir, she has no training? None at all?" Hush exclaimed in exasperation. "None, however she has a lot more intelligence than you could ever dream of having." Maple resisted a snicker and Thomas pretended not to notice but Hush's face twisted in humiliation. "She's the reason the mission failed! She was 'feckin about with her bloody drone thing too long!" Hush shouted. "You miserable sack of rough pig shit. She invents a brand new way of gathering intelligence and you get annoyed at her for using it?" A smile spread openly across Bird's face, it was now her time to badly suppress a laugh. Thomas shot her a dirty look but continued on his tirade. "Her drone is capable of delaying a bomb detonation for two minutes! If you hadn't intimidated her into silence and then rushed off you could have worked together amazingly." Dumbstruck, Hush only gathered his thoughts long enough to utter "Aye sir." Under his breath. With Hush's execution complete, Thomas moved on to decapitate his next victim: Bird. "As much as Hush has his own faults he is somewhat right, you spent too long on the drone. Hush made it clear that time was running out and you did nothing. I'm not going to be hard on you because this was your first ever training exercise but just keep it in mind. Tactics and time are very important." Hush guffawed at the revelation that the most recent shambles was in fact Bird's first. Thomas kept up no illusion of having not heard and turned an angry eye back upon Hush. Under scrutiny once more, Hush dropped his head like Zeus and waited till Thomas moved on to the next victim.

Following a short lull, Thomas swivelled his head robotically and zeroed in on Nitro. "You are team lead, all these problems could have been simply contained by you giving orders and communicating." Nitro's face fell into a forlorn expression and concern grew in the pits of everyone's stomachs. It wasn't often Nitro was without his signature smile. "I sorry sir."

"I'm sure you are. You lot need to work on communication and teamwork more. I don't think you are aware of the stakes here ladies and gentlemen."

"No we aren't, sorry but you haven't told us anything… Sir."
Maple said, just barely remembering to tack a scathing *sir* on
the end. "OK that is understandable, let me educate you then
and maybe you guys will work with renewed purpose." The
group echoed a *yes sir*, indicating that Thomas should continue.
"Deep in the desert in an undisclosed location lies a compound.
This compound is home to hundreds of terrorists armed too the
teeth. They are led by Salim Alquedah, a vicious warlord who
instructs his pawns to pilfer, murder and rape everyone they
see. Recently, Mr Alquedah has come into possession of
nuclear material. Whether he purchased this to make bombs,
chemical weapons or just for fun is unclear. We need you to go
in and clear it out." Nitro nodded, already privy to this
information but every other operator (not including Zeus who
stayed blank as ever) looked a mix between shocked and
horrified. "Why don't a government handle it or 'sommet?"
Hush asked, reappearing from his sulk. "Government too
scared starting war." Nitro said as Thomas nodded. "Indeed
they are, that's why I assembled this team. Now go practice
and do better next time. I'm rather disappointed." Thomas
waved them away and turned his attention to his computer,
indicating they should leave. Politely, one of Thomas's faceless
suits walked in and held the door open for them before walking
ahead. The group traipsed out, miserable after their failure and
began to follow the polite suit.
He lead the group into a small tent with five bunks, ready for
each operator. With his mission complete he walked out of the
tent leaving everyone in an awkward silence that festered for a
couple of moments before everyone settled. With a mad dash,
everyone headed to a separate bunk and began to make
themselves at home. Hush was the only one who dared break
the silence. "If you weren't fannying about with your soddin'
drone I could have done that." He said, sharpening the ornate
knife that had become a newfound extension of him. "I could

have uh- I could have done it if you gave me a little more time." Bird said speaking up for the first time since the training exercise had failed. "Yeah course you could've, your bloody drone would have probably broken down. Feckin' jumped up security camera it is."

Bird briefly said nothing but instead turned a brilliant shade of Vermillion as her rage bubbled over. Voice breaking out in full blown lyrical French-ness she squared up to Hush and shouted in his face. "My drones are works of art! They don't let me down! Trust me and I wont let you down with them you thick *espèce de merde*, Jesus!" Incensed by the sudden outburst, Maple climbed to her feet and assisted in the verbal assault of Hush. "Yeah, sorry but this lone wolf hard SAS man thing isn't going to work just-" Nitro interrupted with a long piercing whistle and a demeaning clap. The group fell silent and stared at him. "Great show of bravado. This not what we need though. Gather yourself and work together. Don't fight or nothing get done. Next time we not lose the exercise. Stop this childishness!" At this Zeus guffawed and turned to Nitro emotion colouring his face for the first time since the group had seen him. "You can barely speak English you Ukrainian coward! Why should you be leading us, telling us what to do. I killed a hundred cowards like you in the war." At this everyone turned to Nitro with sombre faces. They all knew the horrors of the Russian-Ukrainian war and they all knew how Ukrainians felt about Russians, even now in 2025. Nitro had been doing an excellent job of disguising his distaste for the decorated Russian marksman, but that was the final straw. A disconcerting smile spread itself wanly across Nitros grizzled and usually friendly face as he threw a punch.

The punch connected firmly with Zeus's face, who stood there as if a mere fly had landed on him. Glancing at Nitro's arms it was pretty clear that had to have been an incredibly painful and devastating punch, but yet Zeus stood there; merely miffed that

Nitro had even dared to punch him. A quiet moment ensued before being followed by an explosive frenzied flurry of movement. In a blink of an eye the two veterans were wrestling on the ground throwing kicks and punches, whatever it took to hurt the other. Nodding at each other, the rest of the group desperately disengaged the pair from their visceral brawl. Now separated, the two glared at each other panting. Nitro still had a concerning smile plastered on his face as his nose dripped blood into his mouth and Zeus was completely blank as a gash above his eye seeped blood into the aforementioned eye. Breaking free of the firm grip that Bird and Maple held on him, Nitro stretched and made a loud noise of elation. "It been ages since I been able to beat shit out of Russian bastard. That was fun!" He smiled even wider and situated himself in his cot, lounging comfortably. Once Hush was certain the Russian sniper wouldn't smother the Ukrainian, he released the vice grip he held. Dusting the dirt off of his uniform, the Russian walked calmly to his cot and laid down also. His mask of emotionlessness firmly in place once more.

"Tomorrow we love each other. Learn to use equipment and work together." Nitro announced to the room with his eyes closed, still smiling. Bird released a sardonic laugh with catharsis and looked around nervously. She knew her drones were up to the task but was she? To her these people, old veterans and soon to be veterans alike seemed too intense. The only one she could relate to was Maple, who as Bird thought to herself shot her a thin smile, seemingly offering a friendship of sorts.

Chapter Four

After a long and well deserved rest, the group had gathered in one of the empty warehouses and begun to wait for Thomas to instruct them what to do. As if on cue, the hidden speakers crackled to life and Thomas's voice echoed around the spacious warehouse. "Today you guys are going to train before going into the kill house. Learn to use each other effectively and efficiently." The five looked around them, somewhat confused. The warehouse they were currently occupying was a large open affair, dwarfing the group. Yet there was nothing they could possibly train with, it was empty and devoid of everything but walls and a roof. Responding to the silence and confused glancing, a weighty button press came over the speakers and a familiar mechanical grinding echoed off the bare metal walls. Plywood walls rose from the ground, creating a doll house mock-up of a small desert town. The walls were followed by another marvel of engineering, packets of ammunition rose out of the ground and rested themselves on sideboards and barrels. Bird let out a long whistle, impressed, before glancing around, embarrassed.

 Then, as fast as it had started it was over. The silence was deafening as the group looked around, bewildered. Maple was the first to raise the question that so prevailed in everyone else's thoughts, "Sorry, but how are we supposed to train on teamwork if there are no hostiles?" The venom in her voice betrayed her true thoughts on Thomas's games.

Bird's eyes lit up with a brilliant idea. Her emerald eyes shining like spotlights, she turned from staring at the small desert town to stare at the rest of the group. Maple thought for a minute before the idea dawned on her too and her eyes lit up. Spreading across her face was a smile that could cut sapphire, It made Hush nervous and made Nitro smile even wider. "We team up with the people we have issues with, in teams of two. Then fight the other team." Bird said letting the emerald of her eyes creep into her voice. "Perfect training exercise." Maple said, sapphires shining. "What exactly does that mean, what will be the teams?" Hush said as he sighed. "You and bird-" "-Nitro and Zeus." Bird finished Maples sentence and the two girls shot each other a smile that could rival Nitro's. "How will I work with the coward, my gun is a sniper rifle, this exercise isn't designed for me." Zeus spoke up gesturing to the plywood town and remaining blank. Nitro spoke before the girls could think what to say. "They have intel operator, now I do. Come with me. Use settings of rifle to help me locate them." Zeus nodded but behind his mask of numbness lay some annoyance that was steadily leaking through.

Hush knew better than to argue, so he said nothing and checked the magazine of his gun. "Make sure they are still flour rounds, don't want anyone to get shot for real." Everyone went through the song and dance of ejecting the magazine, confirming that it was in fact chock full of flour rounds and then nodding at each other. With this ritual complete, the group were ready to begin. "What about Maple?" Nitro said suddenly remembering the wily shield operator hadn't been assigned a team. "After the Fiasco of yesterday I'm sure Thomas will have place grenade traps in this little exercise, to make sure we don't make the same mistakes. I'm going to practice room clearing if that's okay?" Maple said, everyone nodded in approval and agreement. "That means we will need to look out for them too." Hush said, grit in his voice. Once again everyone nodded. Semantics taken care of, the group split into their teams. Nitro and Zeus, Nitro smiling and Zeus scowling under the surface. Bird and Hush, Bird eager to improve on yesterday and Hush sulky. He still didn't understand why a girl with no experience was thrown onto the team. To him she was just a casualty waiting to happen and he had begun to despise Thomas for it. One fifth, twenty percent of the team had no combat experience. It was an accident waiting to happen in Hush's experienced eyes. However, he had resolved to attempt to help her. He wasn't going to be easy on her, or particularly nice to her, but he'd attempt to train her. He'd rather go through the effort of training her than reap the consequences of not training her.

Running to opposing sides of the town, to houses the groups had predetermined, they began to wait for the signal. They expected to meet in the middle and fight it out from there. Even if this wouldn't be nice because of who they were forced to team-up with, everyone was pretty sure this would be great fun. A single shot echoed across the warehouse, a lightning bolt from Zeus and the group ricocheted into action, sprinting towards the centre of the town. There was a small church there and anyone who could take it would have an eagles eye view over the entire town, practically securing the victory.

Hush and bird were the first to reach the church, shooting into the plywood prayer room and slamming the door shut behind them. They both panted with the exertion of running full kilter and Bird threw her head back in laughter. Even though he would never admit it, the sound made the corners of Hush's mouth tug upwards into a smile. "We need to get to the top of the spire." Bird nodded in agreement and followed Hush as he manoeuvred his powerful body to the stairs.

Running up the stairs Bird glanced at her watch, a chunky Casio. It wasn't expensive, but it was reliable and right now it was telling her that enough time had passed that Zeus and Nitro should have reached the church by now. What was taking them so long was worrisome, either they were squabbling like children or they were discussing tactics for how to take the church for themselves. As if in response to her thoughts, a shot ripped through the plywood next to Bird's head, missing her by a hair. The sudden flour spatter on the wall spooked her. *"merde."* She spat in alarm. Hush looked back gun first and asked "Thermal scope?"

"It's got to be yes."

"We'd better hurry then." Now fuelled with renewed purpose, the pair bounded up the stairs faster than ever dodging four stray shots from Zeus as they went up. After what seemed like an eternity, the two reached the top and exploded out of the trapdoor.

Nitro was laughing. He tried to hide it from his team-mate but he was laughing. "What's so funny?" Zeus hissed, the mask firmly off now he was alone with Nitro. "Your rifle cost a lot, yet it be defeated by spiral staircase." Nitro continued to laugh jovially and clap Zeus on the shoulder. This olive branch was firmly cast aside however when Zeus turned to Nitro, rage blanketing his face. Under this mosaic of rage, hatred and disgust was something darker, Nitro spotted the grimness creeping into Zeus's facial expression and his own smile began to waver. *Something is wrong with this guy,* he thought to himself. Face twitching, Zeus raised the rifle and fired a single shot at Nitro. It connected on his left cheek and left a small deep cut that was utterly soaked in flour. Recoiling from the pain, Nitro raised his own gun and switched to fully automatic. Zeus spotted the small movement and ducked around the corner as fast as he could. The chatter of gunfire and the spatter of flour followed him as he ran to a better vantage point in the town. With the church no longer an option, he only had one choice: a mock-up of a three storey block of apartments. Narrowly avoiding shot after shot, Zeus took careful control of his mind and focused on his goal. Surgeon like precision took over as he threw his old body up the side of a plywood building and onto the roof. As he leapt from roof to roof he heard Nitro run out of ammunition, this was his chance. Up until now he'd been leading Nitro in circles but with Nitro distracted reloading he had a small window of opportunity where he could reach his actual goal. He glanced down and sure enough Nitro's attention was firmly fixated on wrestling another magazine out of his vest. Taking his opportunity, he slid into precision again as he leapt from roof to roof silently. He reached the apartment building just as Nitro finished and looked up bewildered. Hiding behind the roof of the apartments, Zeus glanced up at the church, a strange glint was reflecting from the spire and it had caught his attention. Using his rifle's scope to magnify the anomaly, Zeus realised what he was seeing and had to refrain from spitting in disgust. Hush and Bird were no longer holding defence positions and guns but were instead holding their standard issue binoculars and what could only be described as shit eating grins. As Zeus purveyed the scene, full of vitriol, he spotted a small black object abseiling through the air. Zeus cocked his head in curiosity as the object landed on the top of the spire. Hush and Bird glanced down in alarm and the spire went up in a plume of flour.

Seeing an opportunity, Zeus stepped out from behind the cover brandishing his rifle. To his utter surprise he came face to face with Nitro, who it seems had the same idea. Before Zeus could react, Nitro opened fire and covered Zeus head to toe in flour. Wincing in pain, he ineffectually tried to dodge away from the spent shell casings and flour that was beating itself against him in an unwavering assault. Before he could, however, the magazine clicked empty and Nitro's smile returned. "Truce?" He said, offering a hand. Zeus spat down at him and turned to walk away. He was interrupted by the clatter of something metallic and span on his heels. Spotting the grenade he released a sigh as he and Nitro both went up in a cloud of flour.

Maple traipsed around the corner with a cocky smile, shield strapped to her back and arms full of grenades she must of disarmed from traps. "I got you all without firing a single bullet!" She taunted happily.

Everyone convened in the centre of the village as they dusted flour off themselves. Everyone but Zeus had a smile lighting up their faces. "That was a dirty game!" Hush said with a rare laugh, clapping Maple on the shoulder. Maple said nothing, she just smiled warmly. Now the fun was over, the plywood walls lowered themselves back into the floor. The warehouse was now just a normal unassuming empty warehouse.

The speakers crackled to life once more and Thomas echoed throughout the warehouse. "Excellent work everybody, that was your second training exercise. I was curious as to how you'd react if I left it up to you. Maple, Hush and Bird excellent work!" His tone suddenly shifted back to the aggression he had reprimanded the group with the previous day. "Nitro, Zeus. I expect you in my office immediately, we need a word." With that ominous warning the speakers shut off and the whine fled the warehouse.

Chapter Five

"You imbeciles." Thomas's words cut through the flour soaked men to the very core. Nitro opened his mouth to begin an apology but was cut off by Thomas raising a finger. "Shut it. I don't care about whatever random spiel you have to rattle off." Thomas pulled an E-cigarette from his desk and took a long drag of the sweet smelling death. "I understand your two countries have a past. Not a very cordial past, but a past nonetheless." The pair nodded for Thomas to continue. "I don't give a shit, you get that? Grow the fuck up this is bigger than your countries' drama." Thomas sighed and took another long drag of the E-cigarette. All at once he looked ten years older. "I've received intel that these terrorists have been using the uranium to make new chemical weapons. The government know and aren't doing anything about it. We are the country's and possibly the worlds last hope." Nitro's jaw fell open and Zeus shifted uncomfortably on his feet. "Please boys, grow up. There isn't time for these shenanigans. I want to have boots on the ground in a week." Now was Zeus's time for his jaw to disengage and fall slack. "A week?"

"A week." Thomas confirmed with a nod and a grim expression.

Whilst the boys were being told off in Thomas's office, everyone else was lounging in the bunk room, chattering. Even Hush was involving himself, much to Maple and Bird's utter surprise. "So that was our second training exercise?" Bird asked, still confused about what had just happened. "Aye." Hush said, with a nod. "He just wanted to see what we would do if we were taught our weaknesses and told to train." Maple joined in. "So Thomas was just playing an elaborate game?" Hush and Maple nodded so hard Bird thought their heads might fall off. "When isn't he?" Maple said, as Hush slipped into a deep current of thought. "You know what I find strange?" The girls directed their attention at the grizzled SAS veteran indicating that he should continue. "We've all been given codenames right? So we can't run to someone and snitch right? Yet we all know our bosses full name. It's a bit odd 'innit?" He growled in a heavy baritone. "That is odd, yeah." Bird said, playing idly with a deactivated drone. "Not to mention an awful breach of security." Maple said, studying the crevices in her hands. The three of them sat in silence for a while, pondering the strangeness of the situation as a whole.

Their ponderation was cut short by the hidden speakers in their bunks shocking into what could barely be called life. The cheap tech sputtered and cut out as Thomas spoke but the words were incredibly clear. "Due to new intel our date's been pushed up a bit team. We'll have you in Syria by the day after tomorrow and you'll be taking the compound a week from now. Your next, and final training exercise will occur in the morning tomorrow. Get some rest: you're going to need it." The speakers cut out and left the group in silence once more. Hush looked as if he couldn't wait for a week from now as he gleefully cleaned his gun, The old rag squeaking over the shiny metal intensified Bird's suddenly returned anxieties. Bird thought she had conquered these, but now she knew that two days from now she would be smack bang in the middle of war torn Syria. It felt a mite too real for her liking. As she entrenched herself in her anxiety, Bird realised with a painful pang that she hadn't eaten since she got to the training compound. She had seen Hush eating MRE's but she didn't know where he procured that tasty packet of calories. For the last couple of days all she had for sustenance was the water from her camel pack, and adrenaline. The gnawing hunger was mingling with her anxiety and made Bird feel like she couldn't breathe. Attempting to compose herself, she turned to Hush. "Where can I get some food?" Both Hush and Maple noticed the small tear in her eye but didn't mention it. "From 'ere you just go straight then take a right, can't miss it it says MESS

TENT in big bold letters." Bird nodded her thanks and practically ran out of the bunk room.

A few minutes later Maple nodded at Hush, then followed suit. When she got to the mess tent she found Bird, eating a sandwich, tightening a screw on her drone and clearly recovering from a recent panic attack. "Sorry to intrude, but what's bothering you?" Maple said, grabbing a sandwich for herself from the pile. "It's just overwhelming, you know?" Bird said, sniffling a little and taking another microscopic nibble of her sandwich. "You've really been thrown into the icy end of the fishing hole haven't you?" Maple said, taking a huge hearty bite and spraying crumbs. For a moment, Bird laughed at the strange aphorism and the bounty of crumbs being projected towards her. That moment faded however, and was slowly lost to nothingness as all good moments eventually are, and the clouds fell over Bird's expression once more. "Yeah I have I suppose. Never done anything like this before. I'm just an engineer." In response Maple guffawed. "You are not just an engineer, if that's all you were Hush wouldn't even bother trying with you. He recognises you've got potential it just vexes him that your involved in such an important mission before you can gather some experience." A smile flashed across Bird's face briefly before it was consumed by the tides and turmoil of her mind. "In a week we'll be in Syria armed with real bullets against real terrorists who in turn are armed with real guns. The first time I picked up a gun was right before Thomas pulled me in for this job. You want to know what happened?" Maple gave Bird a caring nod and Bird continued hesitantly. "It had a hair-trigger, I didn't know what that meant so I accidentally killed a man. A disgusting man, but I still killed someone nonetheless."

"We all make mistakes like that, the trick is to not make them to people who don't deserve it." Maple said with a chuckle and a wink. Then her tone fell serious. "I wanted to do this. Unlike you, I've had experience. This sucks, but believe me. Just because you have experience doesn't mean your superiors will listen to you. You've got to prove yourself, prove your moxie and grit and rub it in their righteous faces that you can do it. I know you can Bird. You just have to believe it yourself." A brief smile flashed once more and then curdled. "I don't think I'm ready to kill more." Maple considered this for a moment. Once her consideration was done she walked up to Bird and swept her up in a comforting hug. Bird was rigid with shock for a moment but then melted into Maple's arms like butter. For the first time Bird realised how strong Maple was, physically and mentally. Her arms were knotted like a sailors ropes and her hug held more emotion than words could convey. "No one is. I tell you what, next training exercise I'll help you with your shooting and awareness. It won't help you deal with the guilt but it'll help you disassociate from your actions." With a firm pat on the back, she disengaged herself from Bird and planted her hands on her shoulders, staring intently into her eyes. At first Bird wilted under the scrutiny, but then she rose herself to her full height. Tears still quivered in her eyes but now bravery burned there to. "Thank you." She said with firm resolve. "No problem, I consider you an honorary 'Canuck now." Maple shot a wink and with that she waltzed out of the mess tent, finishing her sandwich one voracious bite after the other. Wiping the tears away, Bird looked at her side-arm. She stared long and hard at the pistol really appreciating its power for the first time. She would have to let this weapon become an extension of her and her feelings and for the first time since she'd been picked up, Bird thought she was ready. She pulled the heavy slide back and grabbed the gleaming bullet the gun ejaculated. Rolling the brass between her fingers she remembered an old Latin maxim her mother had taught her. "Si vis pacem, para bellum." She said aloud, feeling the bullet roll between her fingers. Her accent came out in the saying strongly and she smiled. Bird was young, still finding who she was, she knew this. However, as she stood there in the mess tent, bullet between her fingers and old Latin accentuated by a French accent she finally felt like she could breathe. Like she was finally finding herself. Re-inserting the bullet into the weapon, she gave it a tender kiss and a smile returned to her face. Standing on the glade outside the warehouse that was Thomas's office the two men stared at each other, hard. "I don't like you, you Ukrainian pig. But, he's right. We need to work together on this." Zeus extended his hand, an act he did with great unwilling. "Thank you." Nitro said as his smile returned. Taking Zeus's firm hand in his own, Nitro shook it vigorously, beaming ear to ear. Even Zeus let a small smile slip but quickly smothered it. The bear and The lion had shaken hands and were well on their way to being kings of the jungle at long last. Their reign would last thousands of years (or until one inevitably ate the other)...

<u>Chapter Six</u>

The previous day was such a success that everyone was in a tremendous mood. Surprisingly, the fact that Thomas decided to suddenly wake the group up at four thirty AM did nothing to temper the mood. A great camaraderie was spreading through the group like a disease and it seemed that everyone was suddenly afflicted with Nitro's smile. Even Zeus had a small smirk twitching at the corner of his mouth. After the rigmarole of the wakeup routine was complete, Nitro politely asked everyone to fall in. The group assembled in a scene very similar to the way they had assembled the day Thomas reprimanded them. The mood did anything but echo that memory, however. Everyone was invigorated and ready to throw themselves into whatever card would be dealt to them next. "Morale is higher, this is good!" Nitro practically shouted holding his thumbs up in a gesture of goodwill. "Today I lead training." A chorus of yes sirs oscillated through the group underscored with smiles and yawns. "We do a lot of attack already, this is good, yes? However sometimes we need defend. Today we defend an objective." Absorbing this information, multiple parties in the group raised their hands. Maple was first to speak. "What location will we be defending?"

"A mock-up of a police station."

"How many hostiles?" Hush spoke, his cocky smirk now charming instead of repulsive. "Unclear. Around thirty."

"Thirty?!" Bird exclaimed in shock.

"Yes thirty. We need to learn how to deal with that."

"What will I do?" Zeus said. Everyone turned in shock at the fact the Russian had addressed the Ukrainian perfectly cordially but Nitro ignored it and continued with a smile. "Learn to use rifle in close quarters combat against many." Zeus nodded. "Is that all?" Everyone copied Zeus and bobbed their heads. "Lets begin then!"

It was an hour later and now the group stood in the middle of a plywood police station staring around in awe. Despite the fact that the whole building was made of cheap, brittle wood the detail was incredible. Fake corpses of policemen littered the corridors and the walls were painted to resemble brick. "Does this make us the terrorists?" Maple joked. The whole group chuckled and got back to the task of checking and cleaning their weapons ready for the insurgency. Bird and Maple were absent, running around the station somewhere else in the mock-up. Everyone had mutually agreed that it would be a good idea to have friendlies on the other side of the mock-up than the objective. That way if those holding the Alamo got overwhelmed they could call in the cavalry and pincer the Hostiles hitting them from behind when they least expected it. Once everybody was thoroughly convinced their weapons weren't going to fail Hush gave the signal, a thumbs up to the camera slowly pivoting in the corner of the room purveying everything. At first he thought they hadn't seen it but then he heard the shatter of glass from across the Mock-up and realised with a smirk and a wink to Nitro, that the game was on.
The glass shattered in the room adjacent to Bird and Maple. It was the starting pistol that sprung the two into action. "Shall I drone it?"
"That's the sprit!" Maple responded, watching as Bird confidently piloted her drone around the corner. The moment of triumph was quickly quelled as Bird's expression sunk into the floor. "There isn't thirty that's for sure." After a brief double take Maple asked the deadly question. "How many?"
"At least a hundred." At this response Maple desperately scrambled to relay the information over the ear piece. Once this was complete she turned to Bird, who had just drew her pistol. "Your stance is wrong."
"Excuse me?" Bird said, French creeping in as she got defensive. "You're too tense, you need to relax your muscles."

Bird shifted her weight and immediately felt the strain on her shoulder disappear. "Like this?"

"Yeah that's the one. When you fire your gun prepare for the kick, don't fight against it. Control it. That's a desert eagle it'll break your wrist clean if you're not careful." Maple said gesturing to Bird's gun. Bird nodded and then jumped round the corner, a cat approaching its unfortunate prey. A group of twenty or so hostiles had their backs to Bird and were pushing forwards quietly chattering to themselves. Seeing a perfect opportunity, Bird fired. She got three shots off spattering three of the hostiles cleanly between the shoulder blades. They fell and exclaimed "Out!" However at the sight of their fallen comrades the Hostiles span on their heels and opened fire. Having anticipated such a development, Bird had already thrown herself back around the corner and into the companionship of Maple. "I got three of them, there's quite a few more though." Maple nodded, listening intently. "You distract them I'll handle them?" The pair shook hands and Maple grabbed the shield off of her back in one mighty swoop. Now protected, she ran around the corner and braced against the impact as more and more flour blossomed over her shield. The two parties engaged in a flurry of activity as Maple soaked them with her water jets and they peppered her with endless flour. Hearing this flurry of activity commencing, Bird sneaked back around the corner. The Hostiles were so intent on getting Maple to drop the shield they didn't spot Bird suddenly taking refuge behind the same shield, crouching and shimmying. Bird smacked Maple on the shoulder, a move Hush had briefly taught her in the plywood town, and grabbed a grenade off of her belt. Wrenching the pin out of its home she rolled it across the floor with fine finesse. It came to rest in-between the group of Hostiles and a few seconds later detonated with a mighty *BANG!* Flour coated every single hostile and they all shouted "out!" pretending to fall to the ground. The Hostiles who hadn't entered yet spotted this and made their way to another entry point. With a great laugh, Maple shut off her water jet and re-shouldered the shield turning to Bird. The two hugged in celebration briefly but were interrupted by the rustle of cloth behind them. In an instant the two wheeled themselves around, and came face to balaclava with a Hostile. Bird lifted her hand-cannon and pulled the trigger. Flour bloomed on his chest just as it bloomed onto Bird's chest. In a cruel twist of fate the two had fired at exactly the same time. Both Bird and the Hostile said out and lowered themselves to the ground. Looking at Bird with a genuine tear in her eye Maple apologised. "Sorry, I shouldn't have hugged you." Bird laughed, a little insensitively and reassured Maple "Eh, it's only a training exercise. We won't do that in the real thing. Now stop being such a polite stupid Canadian and go make them regret it." Bird said with a wink, referencing Maple's prior wink. As if on cue, the pair heard glass shatter across the police station and Maple rushed off clutching her shield in pursuit of revenge as Bird smiled after her, covered in flour and hopeful for the teams chances. Back on the point, the men were still reeling from the truth involving the nature of the number they were up against. Even Nitro it seemed, didn't know the insurmountable task they were walking into. In a moment of what could be described equally as genius or insanity, Nitro placed one of his charges on one of the sites walls and began the detonation process. A risky gamble as it would give the Hostiles another entrance to the site (three instead of the two doorways flanking the boys) but if it paid off they would take a group of Hostiles by utter surprise. Much to Nitro's glee he heard at least one man shout in alarm as the charge began ejecting the flashes. The pad exploded, brilliant as ever, revealing a group of ten men rubbing their eyes. All three of the boys turned to the Hostiles and opened fire, refusing to let them recover from their dazed position. *Out* after *out* echoed through the new doorway. Once only three remained Zeus and Nitro stepped back and behind cover so that Hush could have a little fun. With a nod of approval and a hasty: "Thanks lads." Hush rushed in-between the three men. Dropping onto his knees and sliding he went straight through the legs of one whom he mimed stabbing in the groin. "Out!" Now recovered, the other two turned to him and attempted to fire. However, before they could react, Hush had leapt to his feet and begun to wrestle the gun off of one of them. The Hostiles ally couldn't attempt to shoot Hush as he grappled with his friend without catching the aforementioned friend in the cross-fire. So he did nothing, remained inert and let his friend be overpowered by the old SAS veteran. Feeling the resistance to his grip on the Hostiles weapon Hush planted his knee on the Hostiles chest and yanked with all his might. The gun, with Hush attached to it, went flying out of the Hostiles grip and Hush shot the now defenceless hostile as he flew backwards. "Out!" Twisting through the air in a corkscrew, Hush opened fire on the final hostile. Hush accidentally held the trigger too long and was surprised by the recoil. The gun pulled up and flour covered the hostile mid-riff to forehead. "Out! Jesus I'm out!" The hostile shouted, as he pretended to die. By the end of the assault it looked like a wintery battlefield. 'Snow' littered 'corpses' and at the centre of it all was Hush.

On a hunch, Zeus pulled his rifle up and looked through the Electro Magnetic Sensor at the wall opposite to the one they'd just blown through. To his great amusement, he saw that the Hostiles had armed some claymores ready to blow each of the team to bits if anyone got greedy and went over there. He lined up his scope and shot them through the wall. As he did so he heard a very quiet gasp. Fumbling to his thermal scope, Zeus looked through the wall and found the heat signatures of six men. With a smile he raised the rifle and took each and every one of them out through the wall. Hearing a chorus of "Out!"

penetrating through the bullet holes Zeus had created in the wall and realising no one was looking at him, he released a private smile. He silenced it however when Hush turned to him and whispered: "Do you hear that?" Turning his trained ear to the silence, Zeus confirmed that he did in fact hear it. From across the police station the sound of gunfire, shouting, water jets and the awe inspiring sound of metal grinding up against metal could be heard.

In the middle of this epic cacophony stood Maple. She had tracked down the final party of Hostiles and had thrown herself into the fray. Spinning in a circle and soaking them, she swept their legs. A few of them went tumbling to the ground and she mimed hitting their necks with her shield "Out!" the few echoed. Gaining some momentum from swinging her shield forwards, Maple barged out of the circle of men and dropped a grenade in her wake. The grenade exploded in a plume of glory and a plume of "Out!" thinning the group down from twelve to a mere five.

The five were scattered and uncertain, checking for flour on their uniforms. Using their uncertainty Maple smacked one with her shield and winced at the *thump* the man fell to the floor, wheezing, and barely choked "out!" Lowering her shield Maple did what she did in the mall and used the edge to support her gun. *Bang* "Out!", *Bang* "Out!", *Bang* "Out!", *Bang* "Out!", *Bang… Nothing.* Five shots, only four hits. Cursing, Maple barely swung her shield up in time to avoid the sudden spray of bullets. More flour encrusted her shield, covering the original layer. Dropping his gun the Hostile charged her brandishing a rubber knife. Maple attempted to shoot at him around her shield but was confronted with a disappointing click. It was empty. She holstered it and braced for impact. Even though she was prepared, the Hostile collided with her with surprising velocity and she was sent flying backwards onto the floor, dropping her shield in the process. Lifting her middle finger in an act of defiance, she crawled backwards as the Hostile gleefully advanced on her. Just as he was rising the knife to mime bringing it down violently onto Maple's face, a shot echoed to her left and his head erupted in flour. With a disappointed grunt the hostile said "Out." Forlorn that he couldn't take one of the operators out, the Hostile didn't bother pretending to be dead and instead just walked away and presumably out of the simulation.

Darting to her left in alarm, she found Nitro stood there with one hand brandishing his smoking pistol, the other brandishing a thumbs up and his face harbouring a larger than life grin. Maple returned the grin and looked at Hush who had just appeared in her peripheral vision. He offered his paw and she took it, using it to climb to her feet. For a moment it looked like he was going to hug her but instead he just reloaded his gun purveying the carnage Maple had been responsible for. Then he graced her with a simple "Bloody hell, nice job" and a clap on the shoulder. Walking in, still covered in flour from her unfortunate 'death' Bird wrapped Maple in a hug. Zeus and Hush scowled at the unprofessionalism but Nitro internally applauded the two women for their blossoming friendship. With this display of affection complete, the speakers whined to life for the umpteenth time that week and the *'bing bong'* sounded that told the group they had succeeded and complete the training exercise. Thomas's joyful laughter echoed over the speakers. He laughed for a long time…

Unto the Breach
"Regard your soldiers as your children, and they will follow you into the deepest valleys; look on them as your own beloved sons, and they will stand by you even unto death."

Chapter Seven

The group stared out of the windows in silence anticipation. Aside from the faceless pilot they were alone. Thomas had chosen to remain in Scotland under the guise of 'keeping up appearances.' They groups last interaction with him, before the boarded the olive green chinook they now sat in, was the first positive interaction they'd had as a whole. Thomas had sung their praises dazzling them with a brilliant smile. "That was excellent! Only one casualty" At that he had looked pityingly at Bird. "But we can work with that, we certainly can!" With that vague comment he had risen, shook each one of their hands and declared "You lot are ready! I'm pushing the date even closer ladies and gentleman, you ship out now." He had then proceeded to herd the shell-shocked group into an idling helicopter.

Six hours after this event they were still on the rickety helicopter and still processing the fact that in an hour they'd be in the middle of war-torn Syria. The closer they got the more and more the group would swear that they heard bullets and shells whizz past the exposed helicopter. Probably only a figment of their imaginations, but humbling nonetheless. It was no longer a training exercise, they were armed with real bullets and so would the enemy. Messing up now wouldn't mean a reprimand, it'd mean Thomas have to contact the relatives. "Coming in for landing now." The pilot shouted. Staring out the window, Bird saw the dusky blackness beneath them transform into a sea of golden sands as the helicopters landing lights illuminated the floor. The helicopter touched down with a soft *thump* and all five of them stepped tentatively off of the ramp and onto the sand. Walking to a small group of tents that were tucked away, sand coloured and hidden. The group absorbed their surroundings mentally. The fine sand compressing under their boots was both comforting and oppressive. In fact, the entire picturesque landscape was mired firmly in this mood. A beautiful haven of dunes and death. A sudden blast of wind smothered the group in sand and they all sputtered, choking for a moment. The air was full of gunpowder, dust and death. The compound they would be assaulting was three miles to the west and even separated by this distance the atmosphere permeated into the very sand grains themselves. Good things did not happen here.

With their assessment of the environment complete, the group stepped into the tent, shutting the flap behind them silencing the screaming wind and the pain that it conveyed. Nitro broke the newly rotting silence in an attempt to raise the groups morale. "That was long flight, I understand. Tomorrow we plan; today we rest." A unanimous cheer went around the group as they simultaneously crawled into the already prepared hammocks. Six comfy hours later, the hammocks were still full with the exemption of Zeus and Hush. The two had woken after four hours of sleep, operating as finely tuned instruments of destruction. "Three miles that way, there are hundreds of terrorists begging for my bullet." Hush said, gesturing vaguely off into the distance. With a start, Zeus remembered the incredible magnification of his rifle and began to climb the largest dune he could see. Hush silently followed, curious and soaking with sweat as the sun began to rise. Once at the summit Zeus snapped the scopes magnification onto 500x and stared westward. Blurry lines emerged from the fog and he began to probe further, seeing if they were any obvious weak-points in the terrorists defence. "I can see the compound from here, it's blurry but I have a visual." Hush nodded in affirmation, and the two scoured the compound together. They inspected it until the sun blazed above them, slowly roasting them. A sudden shout drew their attention away from the compound and with a start the pair realised how long they'd been up there. Turning around, the pair saw their three comrades milling around the camp making food, small-talk and presumably, plans. Looking at each other and chattering quietly about their findings, the two began their descent and were greeted by Nitro. His normal smile was modified slightly by the addition of a fine sheen of sweat from the blazing heat He didn't seem to mind as he launched into conversation with the pair however. "Morning, we began to think you lost it maybe!" Nitro said in reference to the pairs foray into the compound from afar. "I was thinking maybe later today Bird and Zeus can gather intel on target?" He continued with a nod to Zeus. "That's a good idea, we tried our best and think we found some weak-spots in the wall but we couldn't actually see much. Getting someone closer is important." Hush said, precisely dusting sand off of his knifes holster. Everyone nodded at each other then disbanded, all walking different directions. Nitro bumped into Bird at the mess tent, coincidentally, and she started the conversation with a friendly wave. "Hiya Nitro, I'm warm." She said in a blanket statement that she hoped would disguise her returned anxieties. This feeble attempt was ineffectual and Nitro saw cleanly through the act like it was made of glass; however he chose to ignore it. "Today you help Zeus, yes?"

"That is what you told me." She said burying her face in a water bottle as she took a lengthy sip. "I know you're scared, but he'll keep you safe, OK? Or maybe you surprise us and keep him safe." With this morsel of humour dispensed, Nitro walked out of the mess tent, water bottle in hand, smiling, sweating and laughing. As much as Bird didn't want to admit it, his smile was infectious and as she stood there she felt her worries melt. Not melt away, they were still very much there, but they melted into obscurity. Shoved in a closet, ready to spring on her when she opened the door. Talking a gulp from the water bottle again, Bird mopped her brow. Saying she was warm was an understatement, as a French English girl she was used to the rain not what felt like a slow-cooker. Just as she was lamenting the heat, Maple walked in to join her in lamentation. Maple kept slightly losing the grip on the shield she clutched on one arm as her sweat slicked the handle but she was certainly making a go of it. "I thought night was bad but good lord this is boiling!" She said humorously gesturing to the air itself. "It certainly isn't hockey weather." Maple laughed at the surprising reference. The heaving of her chest as she laughed caused her to lose her meagre grip on the shield. It fell to the floor with a clatter making the two jump before they turned to each other with sweaty, toothy grins. "Sorry about that!" Maple laughed, picking up the now dry shield. "Anyhow, onto what I actually wanted to talk about." Maple continued as Bird cocked her head in curiosity. "I wanted to give you this." She said offering a strange oblong contraption. "What is it?" Bird asked as she took the heavy object in her hand. "An incendiary grenade, I'm sure you'd love the engineering behind it." She shot another toothy grin at Bird and continued. "If you think something's going wrong I want you to throw the grenade and run like hell. After a few seconds it will throw up a wall of fire that no one could follow you through."

"Why?" Bird said, pulling her gaze from the contraption and focusing her attention on Maples eyes. "Because if what happened in training happens whilst we're here, you won't be covered in flour." The implication was clear and it brought Bird crashing to reality once again. "I don't want to panic you, I just want you to have a way to get out if you really have to okay?" Bird nodded as Maple hugged her. Nitro's voice echoed from outside and Maple turned to the source of the sound. "It seems like you've got to go."

"I suppose I do." Bird turned to leave but Maples hand on her shoulder stopped her. "Hey don't worry Bird, you got this." Pulling Bird into yet another brief hug, she whispered into Bird's ear "Hey don't forget you're a woman, these backwards terrorists will probably off themselves when they see you operating a gun." Bird chuckled at the macabre joke and Maple disengaged the hug. Armed with a reassuring smile, Maple span Bird around and gave her a little shove. Taking the signal Bird walked out of the tent, attempting to keep her head held high.

Chapter Eight

Now it was mid-day, and if the sun was playing poker it had revealed it's entire hand. Bird was slow-cooking before, now she was submerged in a deep fat fryer. The sweltering smog, forged by the heat, filled her mind and a cloud fell over her thoughts as she retreated into herself. Zeus noticed this dissociation and internally smiled. *This young French girl may be a newbie but if she gained the ability to control her dissociation she would be a very effective hunter* Zeus thought privately before turning his attention back onto the hike.

Half an hour later and the pair reached the compound. Fog lifting from her mind, Bird processed what lay before her. Approximately six-hundred feet ahead of them lay a sandstone fortress. Towering above the pair, even from a distance, it gave every impression of being impenetrable. However, Zeus knew that no matter how tall you build your walls their would always be a sore spot. A weak spot that, if left unchecked, could be brutally ripped open with reckless abandon.

For a good long while the two crawled the perimeter. Due to their stealthily slow method of travel, the task took an hour that felt like an eternity. Once time had finished melding together into a malaise of monotony, the pair raised into a sitting position behind a convenient dune. "What do you think?" Zeus said, surprising Bird. "Me? What do I think?" Zeus nodded in infirmity and Bird began to fumble for words. She searched through the filing cabinets and drawers of her brain, desperately grasping for the thing that she knew she had noticed but had been stored away in her brain for safekeeping. Bird was dealing with a queer phenomenon that all humans experience. If you put something somewhere to keep safe it's more likely you forget where that thing is entirely in a cruel fit of irony from the universe. This sudden onset forgetfulness was certainly a symptom of her compartmentalisation and she knew it. Zeus stared at Bird patiently whilst she fumbled through her mind. "They weren't many guards in the watchtower!" Bird exclaimed with gusto, proud that she'd located the observation in her mind. Zeus wasn't satisfied however, he gestured for her to continue, a calculated attempt to cajole a good hunter out of her analytical mind. "Uhm… The few that were up there seemed like they weren't paying much attention." A fleeting ghost of a smile appeared in the corners of Zeus's mouth as pride clouded his mind. The rush of unfamiliar emotion briefly threw him off kilter but he quickly recovered his composure. "Good, you were listening. I was thinking that Nitro could blast through one of the walls." Hearing Zeus actually address Nitro by his call-sign instead of by a derogatory insult warmed Bird's heart a mite and she had to play catch-up with her thoughts once more. "which wall?" She managed to say after a momentary pause. "Can it take photos?" Zeus said directly. "Can what-" Zeus interrupted Bird mid-speech with a stare so withering it immediately made the answer clear. "Oh- My drone! Yes it can." Nodding in approval, Zeus outlined his plan. "Use your drone to take photos of the compound from above, Then we take those photos to Nitro and determine the best place to breach from."

"Is that it?" Bird exclaimed, amazed at the simplicity of the plan. "Yes, less complex means less things to go wrong."

The two followed this plan for an hour, Zeus keeping an eye on the drone with his rifle as it took multiple detailed photos of the compound walls and buildings. They had a few close calls where one of the terrorists almost spotted the drone but they managed to squeak by unharmed. As the day continued the sun got lower and lower until it was directly opposite the pair. Beating down on everything, the sun beams had located Zeus's gleaming sniper rifle and he hadn't yet noticed. It was subtle but if you were on the walls of the compound and stared hard enough into the middle distance his rifle shone like a beacon. Unfortunately for the pair, one of the guards had spotted it whilst half zoned-out. Blissfully unaware, the two kept taking photos with the drone whilst the terrorist leaned his rifle against the golden grain of the sandstone parapet. Flipping down his cracked 5x magnifier that he had recently pilfered from an abandoned military base nearby the terrorist located the pair. He could see them nestled behind a dune barely peeking out. Unable to get a good angle, he squeezed the trigger anyway. The old assault rifle screamed into life and a shot cracked across the dunes like a whip.

The shot ripped straight through Zeus's leg, barely missing the femoral artery as it recklessly entered him. On instinct he pulled back his leg to behind the dune and Bird followed suit quickly making sure she was behind the cover entirely. Jaw agape, she stared at the disconcertingly calm Zeus as his blood mingled with the sand. Resisting the urge to vomit, she asked a question that bordered on rhetorical, as ridiculous as it was. "Are you okay?!" She shout-whispered in horror. "Yes it missed my femoral artery, clean shot in and straight out. It's only minor." It didn't look minor to Bird but when he started to crawl away down the dunes and further out of the sight-lines of the terrorists on the walls she didn't question him. Bird called back her drone and pocketed it, still horrified. By the time the drone was pocketed Zeus had disappeared over the last dune leaving behind a snail like trail of blood soaked sand. Resolving to not burn any more time, she followed the trail. When she crested the final dune and reached the point where the pair had been able to walk without being spotted she scanned for Zeus looking out into the desert. She expected to see an injured but tough Zeus hobbling back towards base-camp. Instead she was greeted with an empty horizon and a sinking feeling in her gut. Zeus wasn't hobbling, in fact he wasn't even walking. He lay crumpled on the floor in a rapidly expanding puddle of blood attempting to tie a tourniquet around his wound. Running over to him, Bird realised he was slipping in and out of consciousness. Fighting a losing battle against himself as he attempted to staunch the flow of crimson. Taking a knee beside him, Bird finished the tourniquet for him and evaluated the situation. "Get me to... Base camp... Need blood." Zeus just barely managed to slur in-between the world fading to dark.

With a start Bird remembered her radio and opened the communications channel. Nitro's voice echoed out of the ear-piece but Bird heard nothing over the blood rushing in her ears. "Zeus hurt badly." She managed to prattle off. Grabbing the tag from his dusty uniform, Bird announced Zeus's blood type to Nitro and told him to get as much ready as he could. With base-camp informed she did the only thing she could think of to get Zeus to safety; she heaved him onto her shoulder and began to run...

Chapter Nine

Bird's arms burned and ached but she didn't care. If she dropped the load she was carrying he would die, so she kept running desperately. At some point in the pilgrimage tears began to run down her face, leaving tracks through the sand that caked her countenance. The panic was beginning to set in and as the adrenaline slowly wore off her entire body burned more and more but she didn't care, she had to keep running. She ignored the tears, She ignored the pain and just focused on saving the humourless man that was slumped on her back. Occasionally, Zeus would awaken and mumble something incoherently in Russian; Bird took this as good sign. It meant he was still alive and she wasn't hauling a corpse. Sweat pouring off her like blood from an open wound, Bird resolved herself. She really needed to hurry otherwise she *would* be hauling a corpse.

So she ran. And ran. For what seemed like hours, until…

Clutching five pints of A positive blood and a medical kit, Nitro anxiously scanned the surroundings. His smile still remained, permanently plastered to his face, but his eyes told the true story. A terrible tempest brewed in them as they reflected back the desert. Nitro had heard the tone of Bird's voice over the comms. Whatever had happened was serious and possibly mission altering. If it was bad enough the whole team might have to abandon mission and go home, rendering their training and time utterly worthless. As he pondered this a new thing appeared, reflected by his eye's lenses. Sweating, panting and crying, the small French woman: Bird had appeared over the Horizon. Strung over her shoulders was a lolling Zeus, dwarfing Bird's slender frame in an almost comedic juxtaposition. She dumped him on the floor, rambled incoherently whilst wildly gesturing and then promptly collapsed from exhaustion. Ignoring this strange display, Nitro focused his attention on Zeus. The situation was dire, he had lost approximately a litre and a half of blood and was losing even more as he laid on the desert sand. Nitro screamed for the others as he worked and they quickly appeared peeking their heads out of the tents. Nitro's countenance showed no hint of a smile just pure concentration and graveness. Spotting the two collapsed figures, Hush and Maple dashed over as fast as humanely possible. Hush addressed Nitro whilst Maple inspected Bird "'whaddya need?" He said genuinely, without a single hint of his usual cockiness lacing his voice. "He losing a lot of blood. I transfusing now, just sew up the wound. Exit and entry it was clean shot."

"Thank God." Hush said obliging, glad he didn't have to dig shrapnel out of the decorated Russian marksman. The two men got to work efficiently and effectively, doing everything in their power to keep Zeus living. The sun began to set whilst the men worked, saving them from the heat but thrusting them into the dark and cold.

Whilst the two men worked Maple had determined that Bird was fine and had thrust a water bottle into Bird's hands when she came to. "Drink." It was a single word but it was an order, dehydration clouds your judgement and if Maple's hunch was right they needed judgement right about now. With Bird somewhat recovering from her exhaustion and dehydration, Maple rushed to over to Zeus offering to help. "No just stay out of our way." Hush said, concentration hardening his voice. "Let me help." Bird stubbornly crusaded. Giving in, Nitro turned to her and hastily handed her a bottle of disinfectant. Not rubbing alcohol or anything medical, but a bottle of bleach. Shrugging, she opened the cap "There" Nitro said pointing with his free hand at the wound. "Clean." Eager to help, she immediately followed his order pouring a cap-full of the bleach into the bullet hole. Still unconscious Zeus moaned a little in pain.

"That's good it means he's still bloody alive!" Hush shouted in premature celebration. "Yup, just got to sew this." Nitro said, Needle held between his lips.

Once Nitro had finished sewing the wound, the group (now including the recovered Bird) hauled Zeus into his cot. "Is he going to be okay?" Bird whispered, out of breath. "With rest, hopefully yes. Heat big problem, very likely he get an infection." Nitro also whispered, attempting to let Zeus get some much deserved rest. "If he's careful, and drugged up enough, he can still shoot for us. So the missions not off 'innit boss?" Hush said turning to Nitro, who did nothing except nod in response. Solemnly, the group dispersed and settled down for the night. They lay in their cots, listening to the quiet moans and Russian ramblings of the recovering Zeus. Everyone struggled to get to sleep but inevitably the exhaustion and exertion of the day won over and they all collapsed into a deep practically comatose state...

Everyone's restless, nightmare riddled sleep was cut brutally short by the sound of movement outside. They awoke from one nightmare and into another, someone was outside. More accurately, a group of someones were outside. Everyone, except the injured Zeus (who just moaned slightly and rolled over), bolted out of bed silently staring at each other with knowing eyes. In a moment of quick thinking and fear, Bird activated her drone which lay in her bag outside. Piloting it through the camp she spotted five men, clad in balaclavas clutching Kalashnikov rifles. Bird held up five fingers to indicate that there were five hostiles and continued her investigation. The masked assailants were systematically working their way through the tents trying to determine were the operators slept. "Do they have night vision?" Hush whispered. Bird looked at the faces of the assailants and shook her head. "What about torches?" Before Bird could shake her head once gain Nitro chimed in with a whisper "No, we would see light." Nodding grimly, Hush rooted around in a small locker tucked away in the corner of the tent. He threw off his standard desert-camo clothes shamelessly and stood in front of the group only donning his pants. After a moment of awkwardness, he turned back to the locker and swiftly pulled out an all black set of fatigues which Hush then proceeded to slip into. Now that he was masquerading as a shadow, he strapped a pair of night vision goggles he had retrieved from the locker onto his helmet. Flipping them down, he looked like a strange bug but could see everything perfectly in a green hue. Silently, he slipped out of the tent drawing his knife.

Bird watched from the drone as Hush sneaked up to the assailant that was closet to the tent. Asserting himself behind the terrorist, Hush suddenly clapped a hand over the terrorists mouth and drew his blade across his throat. The terrorist made a quiet noise of surprise but after that, quickly went silent. Blood ran through the rivulets of gold filagree encircling the handle of Hush's knife and he smiled a sick smile, the blade was finally getting some use. With his silent appreciation of the no longer virgin blade complete, Hush began to approach the second terrorist. Who he dispatched much in the same way, silently from behind as if he was an angel of death claiming souls. Despite his rather chunky build, the old SAS man moved like a cat through the night. He silently prowled in-between the tents of the groups makeshift camp searching for the last three assailants.

Following an agonisingly long minute he found the third terrorist. Hush drew his blade across the terrorists throat, hand over his mouth so he couldn't scream, same way he had for this others but Hush's luck decided to turn. As the life drained from the terrorist he lost his grip of the Kalashnikov he was clutching and it tumbled awkwardly out of his hands, hitting an arms locker on the way down with a loud clatter. With a heavy clunk, the other two assailants clicked on industrial flash-lights, revealing everything to them and momentarily blinding Hush as the light filled his night-vision goggles. The final two terrorists took their opportunity and disarmed Hush by smacking him hard in the hand whilst the other grabbed Hush's vice-like arms, restraining them behind his back. Chattering back and forth angrily in Arabic, the terrorists surveyed their dead comrades. One of them spotted the blood on Hush's blade and in a fit of anger whipped Hush across the face with the butt of his rifle. The impact smashed the NVG's into Hush's face, cutting his cheek and certainly giving him a black eye or two. Another symptom of the impact was the electricals failing, the blinding green light disappeared and Hush could finally see those that had grabbed him. From what he could see of their faces (only the eyes really) one was about forty, with the beginning of wrinkles around his eyes. The other couldn't be much older than eighteen, incensed by propaganda and lies the terrorist group probably taught to him at a young age.

They chattered amongst themselves briefly, deciding what to do with Hush. Using his limited grasp of Arabic, Hush determined that the young one wanted to kill him whilst the older one wanted to use him. The older one had superiority so his plan won over, much to the infantile rage of the younger one. Silencing the young boy with a finger, the older terrorist shouted aloud to the camp in crisp English "All of you come out with hands up or your friend dies slowly!"

From her vantage point in the tent, Bird watched the whole situation unfold and a deep panic began to set in. The rest of the group (not including the sleeping Zeus) stared at her for answers as worry deepened in her face. Before anyone could ask Bird what was going on, the terrorist exclaimed his declaration. Everyone glanced at each other briefly before deciding to give in to the terrorists demands for Hush's sake.

Working as a united front, the three dropped their weapons and waltzed out of the tent hands in the air. Spotting the group, the pair of terrorists forced them onto their knees. The older one jabbered in Arabic at the younger one and gestured towards the tent with a jab of his finger. As the young one grumbled off to investigate the group's sleeping tent, the old one angrily rambled in perfect English. "Who the hell are you?" He shouted. "We were just looking for a score and you idiots are just out here, armed to the teeth, in a tent in the middle of a desert. The group silently released a sigh of relief. Up until that point they had all assumed the terrorists were there because of the previous day's folly. They had assumed the terrorists had followed Zeus's trail of blood back to camp to tidy up loose ends. They had got amazingly lucky, the mission hadn't been compromised (at least for now) a raiding party had just happened to stumble upon them. He stared at the four of them probing for an answer. "Well?" He shouted, slapping Bird and staring at the rest of the group. "How would you like it if I hurt this pretty little thing a lot more? Answer my questions!" He shouted in reference to Bird. Rage clouding her mind, Maple stared at the pathetic man who would hurt the smallest out of the group of them and spat at his feet. "Fuck you." She shouted. In an incredible moment of comradeship everyone else followed suit, Hush's spit even managed to hit the terrorist right between the eyes.

The terrorist rose his Kalashnikov with the intention of making an example out of Maple but was interrupted by his younger comrade exiting the tent shaking his head. In Arabic the younger one began to explain *no one else in there*.

Understanding the Arabic, Hush glanced back in confusion, where the hell was Zeus? Hush got his answer as the young lad pulled out a radio and began to explain the situation to home-base. Before he could get halfway through an enraged and confused sentence, a shot ripped through his forehead and straight into the forehead of the older terrorist. Everyone shot to their feet as the two assailants crumpled to the floor, dead. Glancing wildly around, they came face to face with a pale, drowsy Zeus. He was peeking at them through a newly created circular hole in the bed-room tent. Presumably where he had shot through. "I hid under my cot." He exclaimed as if that was explanation enough. Over-exerted he returned to his cot as Bird retrieved her drone and the rest of the group packed up the camp.

After retrieving her drone, Bird dug a small hole and dumped the bodies loosely in it, vomiting several times. The young one in particular seemed to be glaring at her, even beyond death. Nitro handled the weapons, packing them into heavy boxes that he placed in a previously obscured jeep. Hush handled the cots and documents placing them into the truck, resting precariously on the weapon crates. Maple handled the mess tent and their food and water supplies. In her haste she accidentally spilled a gallon of water which was then hungrily slurped up by the desert floor, everyone was so focused on their tasks they didn't even notice this lapse.

Whilst all of this was going on, Zeus sat slumped over in the truck attempting to stay conscious. He knew he was going to be okay, he just had to recover and he hoped that would happen sooner rather than later. He was used to being the hunter, tucked away in a nest out of sight picking off targets. The prospect of being the hunted, a church mouse with an eagle flying overhead, introduced a new emotion to him: terror. Confused by the new feeling, he attempted to process it whilst cleaning his rifle meticulously desperately trying to stay awake.

An hour or two passed, but the group finished packing and all of them mounted the truck. Bird and Maple sat in the back, making sure the supplies didn't fall out, whilst the three men rode in the front of the olive coloured mechanical steed. Using the fact that they were alone, Maple and Bird chattered. Bird was terrified, it had gone from flour and fun to blood and bullets dreadfully fast. Maple was attempting to calm Bird as she repeatedly vomited out the back of the truck as it blazed across the sands. Having panic attack after panic attack, Bird tried to explain that she couldn't do this that it was too much. With a reassuring hug, Maple explained once more that Bird had the potential to be excellent and that it was awful for everybody when they first started, you just had to get used to it. This answer seemed to frustrate Bird more and she shouted "I don't want to get used to it, I just want to make little gadgets!" Her voice had strayed into French once more as tears stampeded their way down her face. Maple absorbed the answer and stayed silent for the remainder of the journey as Bird quietly sobbed.

<u>Chapter Ten</u>

The long pilgrimage across the sands was cut short when one of the jeep's wheels was sucked into the sand. Firmly beached, Nitro hopped out of the driver side seat and declared: "This is the place!" With a smile. They were much further from the compound than they had been before, a three hour walk east would get them there. Still smiling, Nitro began unpacking. He was assisted by everyone, except the wounded Zeus, and the process was much faster than packing it all up. After thirty minutes, and multiple gauzes applied to Hush's cheek to stop the blood from the cut that lay there running into his mouth, they were set up again and ready to restart the planning for the operation.

Pulling out a comically large Satellite phone, Nitro contacted Thomas informing him of the mission's developments so far. Accepting the Briefing with a heavy heart, Thomas instructed them to proceed with the operation as soon as possible and extract. With Nitro's orders received, Thomas hung up and Nitro turned to the group. "Tomorrow we plan in morning, then we take compound in evening." Bird stared around in shock at the nodding heads around her, she didn't feel ready to do it tomorrow. In fact she wondered if she would ever be prepared to charge into the compound. After a moment of fumbling with her thoughts, she managed to choke out "What about Zeus?" In her old meagre volume. Maple shot Bird a concerned glance, if Bird doubted herself too much she wouldn't be of any use, but Nitro ignored her regression and turned to her with a smile. "Thomas informed me that we had painkiller in our medical kit." At the mention of painkillers the barely conscious Zeus lolled his head in Nitro's direction. "What type of painkillers?" "Vicodin." Nitro said, still beaming, as he retrieved the strong painkillers and tossed them to Zeus, who in what equated to a miracle managed to move fast enough to catch the small bottle.

Popping the small orange top off of the white bottle, Zeus downed three completely dry. "You've been holding out on me you Ukrainian bastard." Zeus jested with a strange raspy laugh, harkening back to the petty names he had called Nitro only a week or so before. Everyone stared at the Russian in amazement after hearing him laugh. However he didn't seem to care or notice as he craned his neck backwards releasing a satisfied *aah!* As the Vicodin began to take root in his blood-stream. "Don't fall asleep now!" Hush joked, shaking the Russian's shoulder. Everyone laughed and in the light-hearted atmosphere Bird began to feel herself packing her panic back into a mental filing-cabinet again.

The group took a two hour nap, waking at ten AM and convened in the mess tents sandwiches and bottles of water in hand. Zeus listened intently as he nibbled on his sandwich. Bird had uploaded the images of the compound to an old projector that was in one of the crates they unpacked. The light beaming from the projector revealed the myriad of dust particles in the air as well as illuminating the layout of the compound for the group. As Bird explained the intel an idea formed in Nitro's mind...

The War Begins
OPERATION SANDFALL

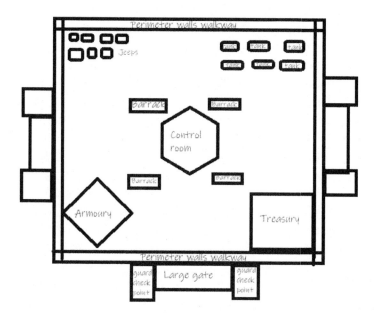

"The object of war is not to die for your country, but to make the other bastard die for his"

Chapter Eleven

"There is weakness." Nitro said, triumphantly gesturing to the wall without an entrance. "We go through there." He continued, jabbing a finger at the spot. Looking around himself he saw everyone, except Zeus, nodding. "Where do I set myself up?" Zeus said, with more vigour than the others expected him to possess. An idea descended on Maple and she gestured at two separate spots on the map. "These guards stations can't see all around right? They just look ahead?" Bird nodded and Maple continued with a smile. "Yeah that's how you guys got so close last time, it's risky but we could place distraction charges on walls next to the guard station-" Catching up and realising her plan with a smile, Hush finished Maple's sentence. "The lads on the wall will rush over all in a tizzy and our lad Zeus can repel up and take 'em all out. Brilliant. Risky, but it's what I'd do." Nitro absorbed the information and turned to Zeus. Cocking his head with a concerned smile Nitro addressed the injured Russian. "They right, it risky. But… It could work. Are you going be better enough to handle it?" The Russian didn't respond with words at first, just a sardonic laugh. Once this was finished, his mask slipped back on and he straightened his posture. Taking the appearance of someone who wasn't grievously wounded only a couple of days before, Zeus loaded his rifle and stood up. "I'm on Vicodin, I'm not feeling anything." Everyone nodded, impressed, then swiftly continued planning. "With Zeus on walkways and most of enemy on other side of compound here-" Nitro said, gesturing to where Maple had suggested they blow the distraction charges. "-We drone out the wall without an entrance using Bird. If clear, we blow our way in. If not, we have Zeus."

Silence descended on the tent as everybody processed the information. Nervously, Bird broke the silence. "Do we go in teams?" Nitro glanced at everyone before decisively turning back to Bird. "Other than Zeus we stay together."

"Too many hostiles to split up, Bird." Maple said expounding on Nitro's short answer. Fingering the smudged brass in her pocket, Bird composed herself. The group discussed the semantics of the mission for a while after that and determined that they should make sure the vehicles were empty first things first. After that they would stealthily push towards the Barracks, submerged under the cover of darkness and silently clear those. Once each of the four Barracks was devoid of life they would take the control room and clear it systematically. Hopefully, with the heart of the compound in their grasp they could take the rest with ease. The plan after that was to situate themselves on the walkway surrounding the glass roof of the control room and make a racket. The remaining terrorists would panic at the sound of shots and rush back, only to be picked off one by one from the roof-tops. Everyone agreed that this was the best possible plan and started to prepare meticulously.

Zeus downed five Vicodin and let the wave take him into hunting mode. His mind was focused and his pain was obliterated. Momentarily, he wondered if he would even feel it if he was shot again but then immediately dismissed the strange ramblings that his mind was engaging him, slipping under the horizon of focus.

Maple scrubbed her shield with a dust covered rag still eager to prove herself. Proceeding to test the water-jets on the shield, she chattered idly to Bird, soaking a wall of the tent. No-one minded however, they were too engaged in their preparations or they were just happy for the miniscule drop in temperature the freezing jets provided. The sun was back in full force again and under the heavy canvas of the tent everyone was sweating, whether they were nervous or not. Once Maple was three-hundred percent sure her shield wasn't going to fail her, she sat down with a satisfied smile, glad she would be judged on purely her talent and not the talent of the technology she was using.

Bird kept fingering the bullet running things over in her mind, sand through a sieve. A cloud of focus had leapt upon her and despite her original fear, she found herself telling herself to get scared later. She could be scared any time but if she locked up in fear mid-mission she would be useless, with this in mind Bird had resolved to force her fear aside and focus. With this mindset, reminiscent of Nitro's, Bird now had the ability to shove emotion aside and focus on the hunt. She was unsure on how effective it would be in the field but was eager to try. Nodding to herself, ignoring the wall of reassuring patter Maple was throwing in her direction, Bird ejected the magazine on her gun and looked at it once more. Fuelled by her new resolution, she analysed the weapon. It wasn't a small nine millimetre pistol like a Glock, it was a Desert Eagle. Bird didn't know much about guns but she did know that the gun she was provided with is affectionately nicknamed the hand cannon. It was world renowned for its stopping power and incredible kick back. Staring at the gleaming silver she wondered why Thomas had chosen the Desert Eagle, of all guns, for her. After she realised she wouldn't be able to reach a conclusion that made any sense, Bird carefully loaded the bullet she'd been fingering into the magazine. Once it was secured she replaced the magazine in its home and flipped the safety off. In a horrendous display of how not to do trigger safety, Bird rammed the gun back into her holster. She knew better than to leave the safety on the gun, but she did it anyway for the symbolism. Her safety was off and she was finally ready to shove her anxieties to the side and fire.

Nitro was chipper as ever, checking his charges and making sure they weren't soaked by Maple's rampant use of her water jets. Once he was sure the electronics hadn't shorted, he packed them into his backpack and looked around the group, beaming. Since he'd taken them under his dodgy wing, they had begun to work together so much more effectively. They might not like each other in all cases but they finally understood that their petty squabbles were unimportant when weighed against what they were there to solve. They were microscopic cogs turning in an infinite machine of death and they were ready to play their part. Even Bird seemed composed now, ready and calm. Whilst Hush cleaned his blade, he eyed up Zeus's Vicodin. He didn't mind the cut on his cheek that occasionally gushed blood at random, that only stung now. He was more annoyed about the bruise that covered his face in the shape of a strange masquerade mask. Smashing the night-vision goggles into his face had been a low blow and it had bruised more than his face. He had made a stupid mistake and it had got him hurt as well as damaging his ego. Even though he would never admit it to anyone he wondered if maybe he was too old for this any-more, he wondered if he was getting rusty. Not one to spiral, he immediately righted his mind and allowed the bruised ego to fester into a calm quiet rage. This wasn't the sort of rage that made a person see red and make mistakes; this was the sort of rage that made a person want to systematically destroy you, to slight you in any way. They had punished Hush for his age and now he was ready to prove how wrong they were. Punish them back.

Nitro picked up the radio, turned to the group with a smile and announced to Thomas "Operation Sandfall is a go." After this he deactivated the radio and leapt to his feet, shortly followed by the others in the group. Everyone's time in the limelight was approaching. Zero hour lay a long hike away. Marching out the tent as a unit, everyone began the approach to the compound, steeling their faces and their souls…

Chapter Twelve

By the time the compound came into sight, it was a monolith cloaked by dusk. A few days prior the sight had terrified Bird, now she walked confidently fuelled by conviction. All five of the group were witnessing the world through the green hue of night-vision, so they didn't reveal their position with flash lights. Their uniforms were all black and unmarked so if any one of them, God forbid, was killed in action their actions wouldn't be attributed to any single government. It was a simple cheat to avoid causing an international war but it also had the side effect of enunciating the eliteness of the group. They weren't just any group of army grunts, they were the best of the best.

Stalking through the dusk like demons, the group planted the distraction charges and walked around to the entrance-less wall of the compound. Huddled against the grainy wall, they were mere shadows. "Zero hour is upon us lads." Hush whispered through his balaclava. With that everyone synced their watches, setting them to mid-night. Simultaneously the group clicked the buttons on their watches, letting them tick once more. As soon as the watches were synced, Nitro pushed his plunger and the quiet compound erupted in noise.

Hearing the sound of the distraction charges beginning their valiant deaths, Bird whipped out her drone and flew it over the wall as Nitro planted a charge on it. Searching around she saw that sure enough the guards on the upper walkway had run over to assist at the site of the distraction. Once he was given the thumbs up, Zeus attached his rope and repelled up the wall, a spider on the prowl for flies. Before Bird could search what was behind the wall they were about to enter through, Hush's impatience got the better of him and he gestured for Nitro to detonate the charge. Nitro obliged and everyone stepped back whilst Bird shook her head angrily.

The wall separated and they came face to face with three stunned terrorists. In a miracle they hadn't called out or fired a shot yet but the time was ticking down before they recovered from the flash and did.

Maple soaked the three and Hush planted a bullet in the chest of each of them just as they opened their mouths to call for back-up. They were in, it was close but the mission hadn't been compromised yet.

Above their heads, Zeus lined up shot after shot and took out the swine one by one. In the darkness they couldn't see their comrades fall and Zeus took pride in the fact that they hadn't noticed their numbers falling away. Five remained and after that he would have full control of the walkway. Taking a certain pleasure in the hunt, he finished the five men. Cleanly executing them. In a mean twist of luck, one of the bodies fell off the walkway and onto one of the jeeps below. Zeus cringed at the deafening crunch of the body crumpling metal. Luckily, the car alarm didn't go off and the guards on the grounds were too busy arguing over each other and attempting to locate the source of the distraction charges to hear it. With the skies secured Zeus got to his feet, winced a little as a small twinge of pain radiated from his wound despite the Vicodin, and confidently walked across the walkway.

Watching the walkway, the four on the ground looked up and saw one of the guards giving them the signal. With a start they realised that the person giving them a signal wasn't a terrorist and in fact was Zeus. He had completed the first part of his mission and was ready to provide support from the air. Searching in-between the tanks and jeeps, the group found nothing but dust and debris. The tanks were armed and ready but didn't look like they'd been used in quite some time. The jeeps, however, were another story. Tracks criss crossed the sand in a crochet pattern and a few appeared to be missing. Once the group were sure no one was going to pop out of a tank and shoot them in the back of the head, they made their way towards the barracks. Clutching their assault rifles, they pushed into the first building and found them all asleep. The group all froze in horror, especially Maple and her clunky shield, they had an opportunity here. About fifty men lay in front of them, sleeping and defenceless. Hush carefully crept in-between them, slitting their throats and silencing them with a glove to the mouth. There was a few times where one or two stirred but Hush managed to silently leap over and take care of them. Once the barracks were populated by no-one but corpses, fifteen minutes had passed and the group were ready to move on. The second and third barracks were both full of sleeping terrorists as well and Hush managed to take them both out entirely on his own. When they entered the third barracks it was a different story entirely, the fifty terrorists that populated it had obviously been awoken to assist with the efforts to find the breach in their compound. Every single one of them was sleepily pulling on balaclavas and shouldering assault rifles. The sound of the group entering the Barracks drew their attention and the terrorists glanced up almost simultaneously. The two parties stared at each other in a moment of confusion before all hell broke loose. The terrorists all stared shooting at the same time, filling the air with a hail of bullets. Hush and Bird both leapt behind an unpopulated bed, giving them just barely enough defence to not be riddled with bullets.

Nitro stayed behind Maple as bullet after bullet bounced off her shield, almost comically. Smiling at the terrorists lack of effect, Maple turned on the jets and soaked them in freezing water. Using the terrorists momentary confusion, Nitro peeked from around Maple's shield and opened fire in a wild spray that managed to hit eight of the terrorists. They had to handle this quickly, the amount of noise everyone was making made Nitro nervous. It was only a matter of time before the other terrorists came to investigate the ruckus.

Whilst the terrorists and everyone else was distracted, Bird began crawling underneath beds and towards the remaining terrorists. Their attention was so focused on Maple that they didn't even spot her slowly shimmying from bed to bed. The only person who did was Hush, who stared at her in utter confusion. Now behind the terrorists, Bird desperately stared around. Finding what she was looking for, Bird picked up the lone assault rifle. As quietly as she could, she climbed to her feet and clicked the safety off. She rose the rifle and squeezed the trigger hard, sweeping it back and forth. It unloaded until it was shooting nothing but the disappointing *click click click* of an empty magazine. All noise stopped and the terrorists crumple to the ground in pain, she had hit every single one of them. Looking down, Bird came face to face with the thirty or so men she had just ripped the life away from and had to look away swiftly. Packing the trauma away, Bird pushed her sickness aside and was proud when she only vomited once. Everyone began to congratulate her for her quick thinking but they were interrupted by one of the corpses raising out the pile and lumbering towards Bird, moaning in pain. Before Bird could react Hush popped over the top of the bed he was taking cover behind and planted a bullet in the terrorists' head. Just like that he crumpled to the floor finally dead, it was strange because Bird could've sworn that she killed him. In the end she concluded that she must have only injured him and pushed on with the rest of the group. As she followed she tried not to think of the agony she had just caused, but it plagued her nonetheless.

Convening outside the control room door, the group glanced at each other one final time. Everyone was already exhausted by the combat but they were ready for more. Smiling, Nitro pushed open the heavy doors and walked in, following Maple's lead.

Chapter Thirteen

Watching carefully from the walkways, Zeus observed the happenings. Those terrorists that had gone to investigate the distraction charge had broken up into search parties and were now scouring the desert, starting with the breaching holes. Surprisingly, they hadn't located the one the group had really entered through yet. Straying further and further away from the compound, the terrorists were out of earshot and all Zeus could see were their flash-lights bobbing across the landscape.

Taking the momentary peace to his advantage, Zeus flipped his ammunition type over to the armour piercing hollow-points and put a round in every single one of the tanks and jeeps' engines, excluding one (just in case the team needed a quick evacuation).

Zeus watched as the group cleared each barrack one by one. They weren't the fastest about it but so far it seemed to be going to plan. Luck was on their side. Just as Zeus was thinking this to himself, the shoot-up erupted in the final barracks and he watched anxiously waiting to see who would win. Calmly aiming down the sights and waiting for prey, he breathed a sigh of relief as the team exited the tent unharmed and made a bee-line straight towards the central control room. He watched the group enter the heavy doors and then turned his attention back to the 'entrance' the group had made in the wall.

Seeing what he thought was a flash of movement, Zeus flipped on the thermal sight and sure enough found a party of the terrorists sneaking through the 'entrance', confusion on their faces. Switching his ammunition, Zeus accidentally selected explosive rounds and dispatched each and every one of the terrorists as fast as he could. His accident worked rather effectively, and by the time he realised his mistake each one of the terrorists had exploded in a gruesome wave of limbs and organs. Hoping that the explosions hadn't been heard by the search parties and hoping that the group hadn't had time to inform the search parties about the third entrance, Zeus turned his attention back to the central building.

Attempting to use every ability his rifle possessed, Zeus flipped on the electronic sensing sight and scanned the central building. He released a long, impressed whistle when he saw how many IED's and grenade traps had been rigged up. After a moment of staring in simple awe, Zeus flipped back onto hollow-point rounds and began the arduous task of destroying the traps one by one.

Much to the surprise of the group, the grandiose doors of the control room didn't lead into a large hall. Instead they lead into a very long thin corridor. The corridor was so thin that they had to form a single file line and slowly shuffle their way down it like kids lining up for a school meal. No doors flanked the corridor, the only way forward was a single door that lay at the end. Eyeing it suspiciously, the group approached the foreboding hunk of wood. A shot whizzed through the wall and struck the bottom of the door, breaking the groups reverence. They stared around trying to locate the source, understanding dawned on them shortly after. It was Zeus taking out a trap. With a sigh of relief the group began to squeeze forward once more.

With a start, Bird remembered her drone and pulled it out. She gestured for the group to stop, to Hush's obvious annoyance, and piloted it through the small gap in the door Zeus's shot had created. The drone revealed the death that waited beyond the door in terrifying detail. Roughly one-hundred terrorists were dressed head to toe in riot armour pilfered from local villages. These armoured terrorists weren't clutching the old Kalashnikov's the other ones had held. Instead they were clutching gleaming M4's and FN-SCAR's which they all had aimed at the door. The antechamber they stood in had two levels, the ground floor and an upper balcony running all the way around the edges of the room presumably leading to the outside balcony. Sitting at the top, invitingly, was a decadent golden door that the terrorists seemed to be angled to block with their body. The ones on the ground floor were crouching behind metal sheets that they rested their guns on, patiently waiting.

On the other hand, the ones on top were completely out in the open. Pushing through the door that opposed the group would lead to certain death, the odds of victory would be so miniscule that if even one of the group survived it would be a miracle. Their only chance was reaching an uninhabited metal sheet for cover.

They'd had many miracles today, why not try for one more? Resigning herself, Bird showed everyone the situation they faced. Everyone's face fell into the same grim resignation that Bird's had. They were too far in now to give up, they would have to go out in blaze of glory. Nitro's smile returned, carrying more weight in it than normal, and he awkwardly gestured towards Hush's flash-bangs in the tight space. With a nod Hush unhooked one from his belt and passed it forward through the group until it finally ended up in Maple's grip. Constricted by the space, Maple shunted her shield to the side and fumbled to pull the pin with one hand. With this done she awkwardly chucked it through the small hole in the door and waited. The group waited and waited for what seemed like an eternity, the three seconds it took to detonate ticking down year by year, century by century, millennia by millennia.

The bang part of the flash-bang echoed into the small corridor and the group flurried into action. Rushing forward as fast as she could in the tight space, Maple burst through the door and into a blaze of gunfire. The group attempted to stay behind Maple's shield and Hush threw two smoke grenades so the terrorists' vision of the group was obscured. Even behind the blanket of smoke quite a few shots hit maple and to her horror they dented the shield; in some places the shots even made small cracks. After the mad dash was complete, the group were crouched behind a metal slab with no-where else to go. Bird began piloting her drone again much to Hush's chagrin and attempted to assess the situation. With a sigh she realised they were in exactly the same situation as before, just in a different location. She'd doomed them and began to break down in tears, Hush stared at her in disgust and carefully pulled something out of his back-pack. "Bloody 'ell woman, have a bit more fight in 'ya for Christ sake." Hush placed the strange contraption on the floor and it clicked on with a quiet *beep*. Seeing what Hush was doing, Nitro followed suit.

"Claymores." Maple said by way of explanation to Bird. Bird didn't recognise the word but could determine from her engineering experience that it was some sort of directional explosive. They'd be sure to take out the first group of armoured terrorists who pushed around the metal slab, but after that, who knows?

Still scanning for electronics, Zeus watched as two claymores were primed. When he realised what must be happening he leapt to his feet with a grunt of pain. Not a single terrorist was on the balcony on the middle building. Now either the terrorists had wizened up and were now avoiding open air, or more likely they were surrounding the group. If Zeus was a betting man he'd bet on the latter. In a moment of innovation, Zeus grabbed his rappel from where it lay on the wall and unfurled the full rope. Swinging it around like a grappling hook he attempted to throw it to the central building that was about twenty feet away and about thirty feet beneath him. It took a few tries but eventually the rappel hooked onto the railing on the control room's balcony. Zeus then proceeded to tie the other end of the rappel to the wall he was stood on, creating a sloping zip-line of sorts. Slinging his rifle over his shoulder he began the lengthy process of shuffling down the wire. Hand over hand. Grunt after pained grunt…

Chapter Fourteen

Finally at the end of his lengthy abseil, Zeus hopped onto the control room's balcony. Pulling his rifle from his shoulder, he heaved it through the window and spat a curse. All four of the team were surrounded by roughly one hundred armoured terrorists. The terrorists were just patiently aiming at the metal slab Zeus presumed that the group hid behind. So intent on their mission the terrorists were that they didn't notice Zeus sitting in the window, clicking his ammunition type over to incendiary. Zeus had noticed that the upper walkway was mainly wood, as were a lot of the sheets that the terrorists on the ground were patiently waiting behind. Aiming for the stairway, he pulled the trigger and a shot of flame streaked across the air, immediately igniting. The newly created wall of fire blocked the way down from the balcony and through the terrorists into chaos. They stared around wildly confused, looking for the source of the flames. Every time they span around to the window Zeus had just shot from he moved on to the next, methodically erupting the barricades in flames. By the time they had realised that they were being shot from the walkway, Zeus had shimmied onto the domed roof. He laid flat and tried to hold his breath as three terrorists, who had been on the walkway that was now being rapidly encircled with flame, walked out onto the balcony.

Immensely confused, they chattered in Arabic and went back inside the building, despite the flames. Zeus had to give these guys credit, they were dedicated. Once Zeus was alone on the roof again, he flipped to the thermal scope and started to pick off the ones who had the best angles on the group. He couldn't take them all out but he could certainly improve the group's chances.

Back in the chamber itself the group sweated, since Zeus had shot everything flammable in the room the flame had really

pumped up the heat. As flames roared and bodies, dispatched by Zeus, fell from the rafters the group felt like they were in the end times. Like the biblical rapture had manifested, contained to a single room. Using the bedlam to their advantage, the group peeked around the slab, careful not to trip the claymores and took a few pot-shots. Most of them missed except for Bird's. Trying really hard to line up the weapon she had hit a perfect shot, clean through the riot helmeted visor of one of the terrorists. The silver pistol rocketed back in her grip making her wrist ache. She'd have to be more careful with the recoil. Continuing this way for a few minutes, she managed to take out four more terrorists. Two of the four rose after being shot once, presumably only injured, and Bird had to place a round between their hidden eyes. Getting bored of the charade of patience, the rest of the terrorists decided to rush around the slab. The two groups exploded instantaneously, going up in a fine mist of viscera. The claymores ripped through their armour like a warm knife in butter and their lives were stolen away. After it was all well and done they had taken care of about half the terrorists but their luck was running dry. Bird's magazine clicked empty, the slide rocketing back to indicate its uselessness. The rest of the group's followed suit with the only exception being Hush, who managed to retrieve an MP5-K from the pile of corpses that flanked them,
Remembering the grenade Maple had given her, Bird unhooked it from her belt and stared at it. It was now or never. She looked at Hush and he nodded. Obliterating her fear and focusing on survival, Bird yanked the pin and rolled it across to were the remainder of the terrorists were torn between their prey and the man hunting them from above. Following a few seconds of nothingness, a wall of flame erupted in a brilliant blaze. Maple, Bird and Nitro all dashed for the decadent door, throwing themselves through with a smile.

It was only when they had the door confidently secured behind them that they realised Hush had remained. Just as they had resigned themselves to go back for him, his recognisable voice echoed through their ear-pieces. "Get that Salim 'fella, yeah lads?" His laugh echoed through their ears and took root deep in their souls. "I'll distract these boy's for 'ya. The bloody mugs 'aint realised your gone yet. I'll buy you time." With that the line cut out and the chatter of the MP5-K permeated through the door.

Crying, Bird turned around to evaluate their surroundings. They were in a small circular room that had a desk at it's centre. The desk was a velvety mahogany and matched the eyes of the bearded man that sat behind it. He reclined in a plush chair, steepling his fingers and regarding them with curious eyes. The bald, bearded man introduced himself in a cheery tone with a hint of an American accent slipping through. "Hello I am Salim Alquedah. I believe you were sent here to deal with me? Honestly I'm impressed that you made it this far." Stunned into silence, the group said nothing; they just glared at him rage burning behind their eyes. This was the man was the reason why Zeus was shot, the reason why Hush remained back there, hopefully still wrestling the reaper. Before he had chance to continue talking in his queerly cheerful voice, Bird slammed a spare magazine into her pistol, raised it and pulled the trigger. Maple and Nitro's jaws fell agape as what used to be Salim Alquedah's face was reduced to a crater. Bird threw her gun onto the desk and simply said "He was responsible for too much trauma." The other two didn't want to admit it but she had a point.

What actually miffed Nitro is the fact that they could have taken in Salim for questioning. Despite the room being devoid of any sort of filing cabinet or somewhere else a document or something could be hidden, Nitro began to search the room. Luckily he found it. Underneath the slumped Salim, in the desk, there lay a seam running the length of the desk. Following a hunch, he placed his fingernails in the seam and lifted. The top of the desk rose, sending Salim tumbling to the floor. The two women whom up until that point had been curiously regarding Nitro, rushed over to investigate. Inside the desk was an armoured laptop and a row of buttons that were indecipherably labelled. Overcome with curiosity, Bird jabbed at one. Maple attempted to grab Bird, but it was too late. A distant *fwoosh* echoed around the compound and the three looked at each other in bewilderment.

Still in the chamber, attempting to take on all fifty of the terrorists, was Hush. His magazines had all ran dry a long time ago and he was desperately dashing from cover to cover, attempting to give Zeus an angle on the terrorists. Drawing his knife, Hush leapt from prey to prey snuffing out their life brutally as possible. Their amour was tough, but his blade was tougher. Three had their helmets raised and their throat slit, two were stabbed multiple times in the gut through their armoured vests and he had cut four of them from crotch to neck. Hush had managed to dodge quite a few bullets but had been nicked multiple times and as he fought, the blood from those he killed mingled with his until he was unsure who's was who's.
So far Lady Luck had shone upon him and he continued his rampage. Then Miss Fortune decided to rear her ugly head, as a large *fwoosh* echoed through the room. Hush glanced out the window and Zeus glanced towards the source of the sound. The Armoury was now in flames, burning rapidly as if it had been instructed to self destruct. The terrorists used this moment of distraction to their advantage and one of them took a shot. Just as Hush was turning back to the task at hand, the shot ripped through his ribs. Grimacing in agony, he felt the entire course of events. The bullet entered, hit a rib (possibly breaking it), then ricocheted off of it, exiting out of his side. Doubling over

in pain, Hush was unable to do anything as the terrorists leapt into action. They grabbed him from under the arms, lifting him off his feet. As he was lifted Hush felt his ribs crunch further and thought *fuck that's definitley broken.* The terrorists then proceeded to hustle the bleeding Hush out of the door and away into the night.

By the time Zeus looked back from the flames he was greeted with an eerily empty room. Frantically, he searched everywhere with his eyes and just as he realised they were already out of the building, a jeep engine sputtered into life. Spinning around, Zeus watched as the jeep sped out of the compound. He couldn't attempt to stop the jeep with a bullet, it would be too risky. If Hush was in fact in the jeep the likelihood of the bullet hitting him was too high. Zeus did the only thing he could think of doing, he switched his ammunition to a tracking round and fired a shot into the back bumper of the jeep. At least then they'd be able to track the jeep. Following this, he activated his earpiece and announced to the group "Hush is MIA, possibly taken hostage in a truck that just left." The other three tried to talk all at once and filled the line with random useless chatter. Zeus silenced them with a shrill piercing whistle. "Whatever you did caused the armoury to burst into flames. Do it again I'm sick of looking at this place." With that he closed the comms and started walking back to camp. As he walked, the jeep that was missing from the compound screeched to a halt next to him. All the terrorists hopped at and stared at the burning wreckage of their former home, horrified. With resignation every one of them planted their Kalashnikov's in their mouths and pulled the triggers leaving a tragic work of art on the desert floor. Unconcerned, Zeus kept walking, confused, they were missing something here.

Still in the control room and further devastated by the (hopefully temporary) loss of Hush, the three attempted to find joy in pressing all the buttons willy nilly. They smiled at the distant sound of every square inch of the compound erupting into flames but it felt hollow. Something was wrong, it was too easy. The terrorists in the chamber could have easily overwhelmed them but instead chose to wait. Something wasn't adding up and it was registering with everyone. Nitro grabbed the laptop from the desk, hefting it into his bag and slammed the final button down. The final button started a small fire in the desk itself and it erupted into flame.

Their mission 'done' the group exited the control room and began to walk back to camp where Zeus and a helicopter waited to take them back home. The search parties had returned and ran past the group multiple times without care. Their main concern was the fires engulfing their home, so the group managed to walk out of the compound scott free without engaging in any stealth, which was a great relief to everyone. All three of them were exhausted, and if they were honest with themselves uneasy. They were missing something here. It felt like they had been given a single piece of a puzzle and were told to solve it. Nitro patted the backpack containing the laptop with a solemn smile. Hopefully that would hold more pieces of the puzzle. Their main priority now was getting back home to Thomas and then rescuing Hush, so they kept walking in silence. Step by step they headed to their new goal.

Chapter Fifteen

Now in the helicopter, buzzing high in the sky, the group felt shell-shocked once more. They were far far away from the original worries that had started when they had first arrived but they certainly weren't worry free. Nitro worked on contacting Thomas, whilst Bird attempted to teach Maple how to hack into the laptop and bypass its encryption. Whilst all this was happening, Zeus attempted to deconstruct the strangeness he was feeling in the pit of his stomach. Whatever was wrong was brushing it's fingertips across his mind but every-time he grasped for it, it slipped away. Grunting in frustration Nitro attempted to get the satellite phone to work. It must have been damaged in transit or something because every time her attempted to contact Thomas it returned a simple hang-up beep and said "Call failed" in a pleasant female tone. Nitro kept trying and trying, getting more and more uncharacteristically frustrated as the technology refused to co-operate.

Dragging himself from his thoughts, Zeus offered to help. He took the phone off his hands and began to inspect it. He reached an awful conclusion, puzzle piece clicking into place, just as Maple and Bird got into the laptop. As they were poking around in the laptop, it received an email labelled with tomorrows date. Opening it, they saw it was encrypted and had been sent to roughly thirty different email addresses as well as this laptops. Fiddling around for a few moments, they de-encrypted and then swiftly read it. To their horror it was a document explaining a plan to kill a man in his sleep. It didn't exactly say kill but it mentioned injecting him with a chemical formula labelled *TEST 8123*. Clearly the intent was obvious. Reaching the end of the document, the colour drained from both of their faces. Attached to the email was a photo of the target. They showed everyone and it suddenly became clear why they hadn't been able to contact home. An hour after the team landed back at base, Thomas had a date with death. His photo smiled back at them obliviously from the document. Nitro unhooked his clasps and threw himself into the cockpit. He explained the situation to the pilot, who then began to fly with a bit more urgency. Time was ticking once again. The compound, clearly was just the start and Thomas seemed to be right about the terrorists making chemical weapons. Little did he know, he would be on the receiving end of these weapons before he could even figure out how operation Sandfall had gone…

Enemies on the home front
OPERATION DOLLARSTORM

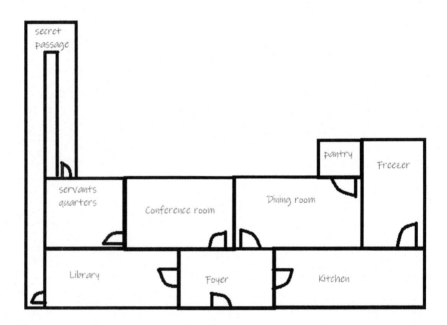

"If a man has not discovered something that he will die for, he isn't fit to live."

Chapter Sixteen

Now on the ground, the team were desperately rushing to Thomas's lavish Scotland mansion. No one had been able to achieve contact with him, and the team were pretty sure the terrorists had sneaked a signal jammer onto the grounds somewhere. So they rushed as fast as they could. The team had all attempted to get some sleep in the helicopter but it was a futile effort, the loss of Hush and the imminent loss of Thomas stood staunchly in the way of their possible slumber.

Squeezed into an unmarked SWAT van, they tore across the Scottish countryside and Maple was reminded of the mission that put her in this mess. The more and more she thought about the state of the world, Maple wondered if this brand new terrorist group was the cause or just a symptom signalling the decomposition of society, the breakdown of natural order. She could swear that ten years prior in 2015 the world had been much calmer, but nowadays people were finding more and more excuses to get angry. People felt a significant lack of uniqueness and wanted to stand up for something, to have a definitive thing that they were passionate about. Prove they were worth being listened to over the other hundreds, thousands and millions who shouted into the void begging for attention. Maple realised she was part of the problem too. Her entire career was a manifestation of this desperate scream for attention. People were too self absorbed these days and in a fit of irony Maple desperately wanted people to stop focusing on themselves and give her the recognition she believed she deserved. Maple was incredibly talented of course, it's just that she wasn't content with knowing that herself. She desperately needed to hear it from another mouth and it was holding her back. If she was singularly focused on proving herself, she couldn't focus on improving herself. These realisations came crashing down on her one after another, like the after shock of an earthquake. Her foundations were cracking and new, stronger ones, were taking their place.

The van screeched to a halt and the team glanced at each other. Zeus was, for lack of a better phrase, doped out of his mind. As soon as the ground medics had seen his state they had pumped him full of clotting agents and morphine. His eyes struggled to focus but that deep rooted stubbornness to continue remained just under the drugged up surface. Due to the nature of Thomas's mansion, Zeus couldn't play it from a long range. Today Zeus would have to push with the rest of the team and make the hunt personal. Some selfish part of him wondered why they were bothering with this anyway. They'd done what they'd been instructed too, it wasn't their job to handle it when the boss was too stupid to not get caught. Before Zeus could focus on the thought too intently however, it drifted away on the wind of opiates rushing through his body.

Bird felt equally as strange as Zeus. She hadn't taken any opiates, but since they had felled the compound something in her had changed. Whether something had broken, or hardened was up for debate, but ever since she wept in the helicopter she'd felt different, colder, like she could kill without remorse. Zeus was right it seemed. She had the makings of a great killer, and the sociopathy was setting in not naturally but out of a need. If Bird didn't lock away all her emotions she knew that they would instantaneously overwhelm her, drag her under the current. She was forcing herself to be sociopathic out of necessity, if she told herself that she didn't feel anything over and over maybe the killing wouldn't hurt her, she reasoned. So she sat there swaying in the van. Quiet as ever, you could mistake her for the feeble young woman who Thomas had selected for the group, but that wasn't the case any-more. Her silence radiated an entirely different aura, a more menacing cold one. With Zeus injured, high and confused Bird was now the most like how he used to be, in the group.

Nitro could sense this shift and it scared him. It seemed like the team was falling apart in every facet and he had no clue how to get them to stick back together. Analysing each of the operators that were supposed to under his command, he didn't see the tough as nails rag-tag crew that could take care of anything any-more. Instead he saw an exhausted group of two men and two women. After the arduous task of clearing the compound and after cutting a dance with death, too close for anyone's liking, they were all shells of their former selves. Zeus had taken a bullet and through a haze of painkillers was questioning himself constantly. He was discovering that he wasn't a true sociopath but instead he was someone who hid their emotions to protect themselves. Zeus had to resist the urge to call himself pathetic when he dropped the mask and felt the crescendo of years of repressed emotion smother him. He was slowly working through it and would surely be better after it was sorted but the battle was taking a clear toll on his mental faculties.

Nitro was glad Zeus was working through his issues (for his sake as much as Zeus's) but he was worried that the instability would distract Zeus more than he already was because of the opiates. Turning his attention to Bird, Nitro was even more concerned. She looked enraged and after the display with Salim he got the feeling she would be a loose cannon. She had found her confidence in the wrong way and was using it to fuel her unhealthy habit of repression. Glancing over at Maple, Nitro was glad to see at least one of his team who seemed to have it together. Dark circles ringed under her eyes, a symptom of her lack of sleep but other than that her exterior gave no signs of the mental maelstrom that was occurring inside her mind. Nitro smiled at her and then turned his attention inward, had he failed? He was supposed to be the team lead and as he sat there surrounded by operators who were in the midst of an epiphany, a breakdown or both he wondered if he could have prevented this. Maybe he was too nice he wondered, maybe he could have kept them on a tighter leash he questioned. Before he could follow that line of thought any longer, the van screeched to a halt and the driver announced their arrival at Thomas's mansion with a simple "Good luck."

Chapter Seventeen

The group exited the van and traipsed towards Thomas's mansion. There hadn't been enough time to properly plan and strategise so the team had chosen to adopt an all guns 'a' blazin' approach. The time for stealth was over and the time for loud and proud was now. Spinning out a little, the van speeded out of the grounds. Its headlights casting brilliant beams of light across the air, revealing millions of specks of dust that danced and drifted. When the team had first been chosen they had felt like that dust. Not special, not unique, one cog in a machine way beyond their understanding. The more they saw, the more they began to wonder if actually if it was more personal than that. It seemed like humanity as a whole was teetering on the edge of destruction and they were the final front stopping this doom.

They reached the door and the flash-lights strapped to their guns bathed it in a pool of light. Nitro mustered all his strength and kicked it. It didn't break at first, but on the third it flew open with a mighty bang; the very hinges themselves separating from the door frame. Sweeping their flash-lights over the foyer bathing it a sickly glow, the team found nothing. Light's revealing tastefully modern interior design, they continued their search. After a moment or two of investigation, the group found the way forward. Conveniently they had four options, four doors. *Split up* Nitro signalled. Everyone followed orders except Bird who stood there debating whether to argue or not. Choosing not to, she pushed into her room, ignoring how monumentally stupid splitting up felt.

Nitro's room was a tasteful library. Books ran along the walls in hexagonal bookcases. These bookcases encircled a pair of incredibly comfy looking chairs. Nitro wondered if Thomas had done the decorations himself, but before he could pursue that train of thought further, he saw it. On closer inspection, the books seemed barely used. All, except one, were coated in a smothering layer of dust. Ian Fleming's *casino royale* shone out from the bookcases, a beacon amongst the dust. Following a hunch, Nitro attempted to grab the book off of the shelf. It didn't budge. Harnessing all of his inner finesse, Nitro grabbed the book and yanked as hard as possible. It didn't break free, but instead it swung down and a door cracked open to the left of him, hidden in a gap between bookcases. Beaming at the cliché, Nitro slipped through the doorway and into the unknown.

On the other side of the house, Maple had found herself in the kitchen. Gleaming white reflected from every angle as she swept her torch over it. As she swept the room for any sign of anyone she came face to face with a man in black. Making a sort of muffled noise of surprise, the man fumbled for a knife and drew it threateningly. Seeing the knife, Maple did the only thing she could think of. She charged directly at him. She hoped the Shield would bulldoze him to the ground and she could handle him from there, but instead he surprised her by placing one hand on the shield and using her momentum to pivot himself around. Mid pivot he managed to slash at Maple's leg. The blade got through her trousers and left a shallow stinging along her thigh. Once again displaying a high tier of training, the man in black hooked his foot around the base of the shield and twisted his hips. The shield clattered to the floor, dragging Maple with it. Maple groaned and then evaluated her situation, the shield was getting in her way here. She'd have to learn the best times to use it and this certainly wasn't the best time for a clunky, hard to manoeuvre, object. Disengaging the straps, she bravely climbed to her feet. Regarding her with curious, emotionless, eyes the man in black waited for her to make the first move. Taking a risk, Maple unhooked her pistol from the heavy leather holster and raised it. Seeing the movement as his cue, the man rushed towards her in a dash to stab her before she could shoot him. Thinking back to the first training exercise, Maple remembered the way Hush would drop to one knee whilst shooting to confuse the enemy. She followed in his footsteps, dropping to one knee and surprising the man in black. He tripped over her foot and went cartwheeling over Maple's head in a grim display of slapstick comedy. Spinning around, she placed a round in the man's chest before he could recover. The shot broke the spell of silence that was over the house and as her ears rang Maple could hear distant assailants shouting in confusion. In a desperate dash, Maple looted the man's corpse. She didn't find the vial, instead she found an empty notebook and a pistol that was tucked into the back of his belt. The sight of the gun sent a small pang through Maple's heart. He could have drawn his gun at any point and killed her with ease, yet he didn't. Maple didn't know if this was because he didn't want to risk spending time fumbling for his gun, or what. Perhaps it was the symptom of a deep seated moral code, the man had wanted to give her a fair fight. Maple found herself getting infuriated at the thought to and had to make an active effort to halt it, the man was just trying to be honourable (assuming he didn't shoot her out of fairness). Suddenly stricken with emotion, Maple tutted and headed towards the door that branched off from the kitchen. It lead nowhere but a freezer, and so she walked out of the house to wait for the rest of the team on the lawn.

Chapter Eighteen

In the dining room, Bird drummed her fingers against her gun impatiently. She had heard movement of the other side of a door that she hoped was a pantry and was now waiting for whomever it was to come through the door. Her impatience built and built until it crescendoed with her resolving to open the door. Throwing it open, gun extended, she came face to face with Thomas. He was clutching a shotgun to his chest, still clad in blue stripey pyjamas. Confusion wrote across his face as he realised why he wasn't being shot at. "Bird?" He hissed. She nodded and Thomas regained his facade smoothly. "I didn't know you guys would be back from Syria so soon. How'd it go?" Bird then proceeded to explain everything as concisely as she could, jarred by the strange circumstances. During the explanation, Thomas slipped into a deep thought. He made small noises of affirmation every so often, especially at the mention of Salim, but other than that he remained silent. Slightly out of breath, Bird finished her recount of the events so far and regarded Thomas with impatient eyes. She was sick of the complete and utter breakdown of communication that this mission had brought so far. The cynical part of her mind couldn't help but fret about Thomas. A wiry bookish man, he wasn't exactly the peak of physical prowess and she worried that he would slow them down. However, the newfound, colder, side of Bird hoped he would slow them down. That way she could practise the hunt for Hush's inevitable rescue. However, both of her thought paths were sturdily blocked without her knowledge.

Everyone has grandiose dreams but very few people tend to practise what they preach. Thomas however was the exception, ever since he was a little boy he had wanted to be an action hero. So when he amassed enough money, he hired a personal trainer. He wasn't useless in a gunfight and as he stood there; scared smirk spreading across his face and a loaded shotgun cradled in his grip, he felt excitement begin to build inside of him. He was ready to prove that he was more than the team's nerdy boss.

Missing Thomas's seemingly newfound confidence, Bird contacted the rest of the team informing them of the mission's developments. Maple was the only one to respond, the other two stayed silent. Turning to Thomas, concerned, Bird suggested that she got Thomas out of the building then went back in to look for the elusive Ukrainian and Russian. "That is absolutely ludicrous. We go look for the fellows together, I already lost one I am not losing another." Bird opened her mouth in an attempt to interject but was rudely shut down by Thomas once again. "I can handle myself I assure you Bird." To accentuate his point he cocked the shotgun, ejecting a shell. Then he smoothly plucked the shell out of the air with two fingers before reloading the gleaming red cartridge back into the gun. Impressed by the flair, Bird stayed silent and followed Thomas. His regular awkward, lanky body language was replaced by something new. More confident in himself, he rose to his full height and walked out of the room; staring down the iron sights of his shotgun with Bird in tow.

Lost in the winding passages, Nitro flicked his flash-light on and followed the sound of shuffling. His light exposed pipe and brick, doing nothing to ease his creeping dread. Attempting to contact the others had resulted in nothing except deafening static over his radio, he had no signal. The passage was just wide enough for the broad shouldered Nitro to fit through however it was still claustrophobic and damp as condensation dripped from the ceiling. Simultaneously radiating a sense of wonderment as well as spine-tingling terror, the passage was a wonderful juxtaposition. Nitro smiled at the cliché of secret passages through the walls hidden behind a book shelf but in his eyes burned something else. Yes this passage was intriguing, but there was someone far ahead. Someone who, by what amounted to a miracle, hadn't noticed Nitro and his penlight tailing him. Nitro couldn't see the mystery person, but he could hear him far ahead sneaking through the passage ways. Nitro wasn't a betting man, but if he was he'd go all in on the mysterious sneak being the terrorist that held the serum (if it was a terrorist and not an insane servant or something else mundane.) After a short while Nitro heard a door swing quietly open then quietly shut ahead of him. He was now alone in the passage… Breaking into the quietist sprint he could manage, Nitro dashed down the passage attempting to close the gap between him and the departed mystery person. Reaching what appeared to be a flat wall, Nitro fondled around the surface looking for the way to open it. His groping hands found a seam and when he planted his fingernails in the seam the wall swung open. The only indication that the door had opened once again was a quiet *squeaak* and Nitro's smile widened. With any luck, the mystery man wouldn't be aware that they were followed. Dancing his penlight around the surroundings, Nitro realised he was in an old fashioned servant's quarters. Roughly ten beds flanked the walls all occupied. Under each and every cover was a bulge in the shape of a person, confirming his grim suspicion Nitro strode over to one. Pulling back the covers, Nitro came face to face with a servant. She had her throat slit and the grim smile had spattered all over the linens. Nitro thought that they was a dark joke in there somewhere, something about a servant never being caught dead in dirty linens perhaps. Briefly distracted, he attempted to think of more punchlines but ultimately decided it was in poor taste and turned his mind back to the task at hand. Possessing more knowledge now, a cursory glance at the other beds told him all he need to know. Every single servant had their throat slit whilst they were sleeping, much like the team had done to three of the barracks in Syria. Grimacing, Nitro pushed forwards and towards the only door in the room.

Striding through the door, Nitro ended up staring directly at Zeus. Zeus was currently occupied with two terrorists on a conference table. T

They were wrestling back and forth like children in a playground. Urgently and confusedly, Nitro stared around looking for the guns (Zeus's as well as the terrorists). The three men were brawling like children when they should have been shooting at each other. After a few moments, Nitro spotted the guns haphazardly piled up in a corner like they'd chosen to dispose of them. Mortified and somewhat frustrated, Nitro turned his attention back to the fight. Having spotted that Zeus was bleeding, the one on top (who had only recently joined judging by his lack of damage) kept jabbing him in that spot whilst Zeus bloodied and pulped the one under him with his fists. The dirty tactics were clearly rather effective on Zeus as with every jab he released a small animalistic growl. The dirty play resurrected Nitro's smile. He wasn't going to ruin Zeus's fun but he'd certainly make life easier for him, even the odds a little. Sneaking up to the one on top, Nitro reeled his fist back. Sending it flying forwards it connected with the less beat up terrorists with a crack like a whip. Taking his opportunity, Zeus quickly arched his back, sending the terrorist slumping off of the table and onto the floor and allowing Zeus to continue beating the terrorist beneath him. Now on the floor, the terrorist (who Nitro assumed was the one he had been following) attempted to reach into his pocket. He pulled out a long thin glass cylinder with a needle attached to it and crumpled to the floor before he could use it. The cylinder clattered out of his grip and rolled over to the curious Nitro, who retrieved it. Staring at the strange cylinder Nitro saw that it was full of a magenta liquid that bubbled like soda but poured around the interior of the cylinder like treacle.

Whilst Nitro was distracted, the terrorist who was being beaten by Zeus landed a lucky shot. His flailing limbs struck Zeus directly in the gunshot wound and he rolled off the table clutching his chest. Able to have a short breather, the terrorist stumbled to his feet and towards the gun pile. Realising what was happening, Nitro looked up from the cylinder to the terrorist and then back again. Internally he shrugged and planted the cylinder into the terrorist's neck. Pushing down the plunger, Nitro pushed half of the cylinder into the terrorist whilst he objected violently in Arabic, seemingly terrified. Removing the syringe, Nitro stared at the terrorist who seemed to have resigned himself. Calmly, the terrorist righted one of the tipped dining chairs and planted himself down. Climbing to his feet, Zeus inspected the terrorists and spotted Nitro for the first time. Offering a strange smile to Nitro he sauntered over to his rifle.

Zeus was missing a few teeth, definitely had a broken nose and profusely bled from his temples. Nitro regarded him, disgusted that he hadn't just used his gun. Turning back to the injected terrorist, Nitro realised that he was slumped in the chair giving every impression of being a corpse. In a risky manoeuvre Nitro approached the man and took his pulse. It was sluggish but still going. Nitro had thought the syringe had held poison but if he was right the terrorist would have been long dead by now. Utterly confused, Nitro attempted to wake the terrorist whilst Zeus fruitlessly attempted to rub the blood off of his face. Realising that softly shaking him wasn't going to work, Nitro shone his penlight directly into the terrorists face. Like a shot his eyelids peeled open revealing eyes that looked like they had been sanded. Red and raw it was like the terrorist had been crying and then rubbed salt into his eyes and as he looked around, breathing heavily, spittle began to escape his mouth and build up at the corners of the mouth. Standing still in shock, Nitro stared as the terrorist spotted Zeus. Zeus was too occupied with his face and didn't spot the new attention so he was taken by surprise when the terrorist rushed at him. Breathing and foaming inhumanely, the red eyed terrorist wrangled Zeus's gun out of his grip before he could fumble it up to fire. Like a deer in headlights, Nitro watched uselessly as the terrorist clawed at Zeus, even attempting to bite him at one point. Just when it looked like Zeus was about to lose control of keeping the terrorist at bay, the door to the conference room was kicked open and Thomas rushed through valiantly with Bird in tow.

Spotting the shotgun, Nitro opened his mouth to object to the danger but no noise came out. Thomas swiftly evaluated the situation and lined up the shot. He squeezed the trigger firmly and the bang echoed throughout the conference room, making everyone's ears ring briefly. As it turns out Nitro hadn't needed to worry at all, Thomas's weapon wielding was excellent and his pellet spread was immaculate. Every single shotgun pellet had entered the mad terrorist's head sending him straight to floor, finally relinquished of his heartbeat. Not a single pellet had missed the terrorist or grazed Zeus. With his mission completed, Thomas barked a simple "Boy's we are getting out of here. Now!" and rushed out. Bird stared at the dead terrorist in awe, still amazed that Thomas was as deft a hand with a weapon as he was. Her worship complete, she rushed out in pursuit of Thomas leaving the Zeus and Nitro alone.

"Why the hell did you no use your gun?" Nitro spat. "It was a gentlemen's agreement, you wouldn't understand-" Zeus paused for a minute debating whether to continue, his abrasive side won over and he continued. "-would you? All you Ukrainian's are dishonourable cowards!" Zeus said, thoroughly breaking down the shaky relationship that been formed by the pair out of necessity. "I am no coward." Nitro said evenly, a threatening smile spreading across his face. "Yes you are! When that terrorist went insane you just stood there! Did nothing to help! Fucking Ukrainians." Zeus shouted, spitting the last word like it was a curse. "I am no coward." Nitro repeated, increasing his volume. Zeus then proceeded to throw a few dozen more childish insults at Nitro. After the third remark about the war Nitro snapped. Flame behind his eyes and eerie smile across his face, he walked up to Zeus and slapped him across the face, hard. Zeus winced at the impact reverberating through his broken nose but stubbornly remained standing as Nitro verbally beat him. "I am no coward. If anyone is coward is you! I was front line, I endured that shit! You were sat up a hill or up a tree like squirrel! Yes you did well, don't you dare call me a coward you not tough you just little boy who's daddy didn't love him enough." At the final remark rage flashed behind Zeus's eyes and he leapt upon Nitro, fists swinging. The two scuffled on the floor, fully reverted back their original dynamic. In both of their eyes the world threatening mission was complete and they could stop shoving aside their obvious dislike for each other. The stakes were lower and they could be selfish up until Hush was rescued, then they never need speak to each other again. The pair both landed excellent hits on each other before Nitro brought the childishness to an impromptu end by whipping out his pistol mid scuffle. Keeping the safety on, Nitro rose the pistol to Zeus's head. "Bang. That why you pull out gun in fight like that. It how you survive. If I no here he would have killed you." Nitro said, climbing to his feet and gesturing to the still unconscious terrorist he had retrieved the syringe from. "Whatever." Zeus replied, climbing back to his feet and attempting to wipe away the fresh blood coating his face had amassed. This achieved nothing, except embarrassing himself more as he smeared blood across his face. Frustrated, he stormed out of the dining room, shooting the unconscious terrorist as he left. Shaking his head, Nitro waited a few minutes then left in pursuit of him, cradling the glass syringe in his hands.

Chapter Nineteen

Everyone convened on Thomas's lawn. What used to be perfect utopia of excellent rolling green was now a muddy wasteland, criss crossed with tire tracks and myriads of footprints. Herding everyone into a top of the range Hummvee, that he had pulled out of his garage, Thomas took the role of leader. Turning the engine on was an anticlimactic affair. Instead of the regular growl of a normal environment destroying Hummvee, the group were greeted with the a quiet buzz. Seeing their expressions Thomas laughed. "I had it converted to electric." He muttered by way of explanation. With the group offering no further conversation, he politely grumbled and turned his eyes forwards. As quiet as church mice, they sped out of Thomas's garden and towards the city. The only sound the group could hear was the tires on the road and the quiet hum of the electric motor. No one questioned the strange direction they were driving in, everyone was too focused on their 'evolutions' or 'de-evolution' in Nitro and Zeus's case.

Thomas didn't seem focused on anyone, at the beginning of the drive he tried to make idle chit-chat but as soon as he realised the others weren't going to reciprocate he shut up and focused on the road.

By the time they reached the city it was morning and early rush hour was in full swing. Thomas weaved in an out of traffic, illegally, the best he could in the giant HummVee. Eventually, after a few near misses with crashes, the group arrived at the white collar district and pulled up next to an unassuming skyscraper. "Bird tells me you tracked the vehicle they took Hush in. Is that correct Zeus?" Thomas said, turning back to them for the first time since the beginning of the lengthy drive. Zeus nodded and pulled out a small field tablet. He turned it on and handed it to Thomas, pointing a blinking red dot. "That is where the jeep that took Hush is."

The dot was smack bang in the middle on an industrial district fifty miles away. "How did they get the car over here?" Thomas asked. Zeus shrugged. "Maybe a ferry?"

"Or maybe terrorist found stupid bullet in back bumper and tossed it." Nitro piped up.

"Both of you raise good points, despite your childishness. Mind if I borrow that?" Thomas sighed, gesturing to the tablet. Zeus handed it over and Thomas thanked him, stowing the tablet in a deceptively deep robe pocket. Still in his blood soaked pyjamas, he looked a right state but instead of his regular geekiness he radiated a confident air that forced everyone to listen and stifled their urges to laugh. "I go in there alone okay?" He said, gesturing to the bland skyscraper to his side. Nitro and Maple began to protest but he silenced them with a raised finger. "I know, I want to bring you in ladies and gentlemen. Show you off, the whole ten yards, but look at you. You all look like you picked a fight with a brick wall and lost. You wouldn't make the best impression I'm afraid. Just wait here, I will be no more than half an hour." The group didn't know who Thomas was trying to impress but they had to admit, looking around each other, that he was right. Even the two that weren't bleeding from several places were bruised all over and had deep rings of exhaustion around their eyes. Before they could respond, however, Thomas rushed out of the car and round to the boot.

Flinging open the HummVee's boot, Thomas retrieved what he affectionately called his: 'emergency suit' and threw it on, discarding the bloody and ripped dressing gown. Now that he was somewhat presentable, Thomas grabbed the tablet from the dressing gown, mustered his confidence and sauntered into the skyscraper. The receptionist recognised Thomas and waved him through, handing him a key-card. Once in the lift, Thomas scanned the key-card on a hidden sensor. It beeped and revealed another set of elevator controls hidden behind a panel that slid effortlessly away once the key-card was scanned. Selecting what was actually the real penthouse, Thomas sailed to the top and stepped out with a sigh. Last time he was here was when he had requested to make the team in the first place, it had required a lot of finesse to word the agreement in a way that didn't incriminate either of them; but after a while the contract was written up. Thomas hoped it would go the same way this time, but as he walked between chintzy marble structures, accented in gold, that led to the penthouse; he began to get an uneasy feeling that it wouldn't.

Finally through the door, Thomas engaged in a meeting with a portly man squeezed into an expensive suit. From behind his desk, he regarded Thomas with eyes that searched every inch of Thomas's face. "Morning Sir, we need a budget extension I'm afraid." Thomas said, awkwardly. At first the man didn't respond, instead he uncorked an old bottle and poured himself a large glass of cognac. He offered one to Thomas who graciously took the glass and uncharacteristically gulped it down. Finished, he flipped the glass over and planted it back onto the man's desk. "Are you alright old chap? I thought you weren't a drinker?" The man said in response to Thomas's little display. "I'm not usually but last night was long." Thomas said, resisting the urge to belch. "As I was saying Mr Agemmeon, we really require a tad more budget."

"And what would you consider a *tad*?"

"At least another two-hundred thousand." An amused expression fell over Mr Agemmeon's countenance as he stared at Thomas over steepled fingers. "On top of the two million we already gave you?" Mr Agemmeon said, raising his eyebrows. Thomas thought if the man rose them any more than he already had they might escape his forehead altogether. Suppressing a chuckle, Thomas feigned confidence and powered forwards reciting a speech he'd obviously rehearsed in his head on the drive. "Mr Agemmeon, I know the government has already given a considerable amount-" Mr Agemmeon uttered a quiet *damn right we have* under his breath, but other than that allowed Thomas to proceed. "-and I know it's pain for you because you've got to route the money through shell companies and the like-"

"To avoid starting a bloody war!" The man yelled passionately spilling a mite of his drink onto the fine desk. "-to avoid starting a war, exactly your right. However surely the knowledge that my team can handle things makes that faff worth it? Especially when what they are handling pertains to nuclear material and if rumour is to be believed, chemical weapons." The man took a long sip of his drink and stared at Thomas halfway between disbelief and appreciation for Thomas's confidence. "Well you can't handle it can you old chap?" He said after a short pause.

"Exactly this is wh- wait what? Why can't I handle it?"

The man pulled a futuristic remote from under his desk and pressed a button. A panel of his wall slid away to reveal a large screen. Tapping away on the remote, the man brought up an image of the compound. It lay in tatters, all that remained (and even then just barely) were the walls. "After you brought your team in, the locals got their own back. Razed the place properly to the ground-"

"Exactly, we did what the contract said, we took down the compound and Salim." Thomas stammered, nervously interrupting. Mr Agemmeon silenced Thomas with a raised finger. "-If you'd let me finish please?" Thomas nodded his apology and allowed Mr Agemmeon to continue his spiel.

"Thank you. Anyway as I was saying, the locals tore the place apart. Stole and killed everything they could find, it's only fair that they get their own back you see?" The man clicked another button on his remote and a news report popped up. A pale British woman, who was understandably melting in the desert heat, stood in front of the ruins of the compound clutching a microphone. "Today I am here at what used to be called death valley, despite the fact that it isn't located in a valley." She gestured behind her at the civilians smashing the place up, voice tinny out of the speakers. "From what we could gather so far, the citizens of this fine country have staged an uprising against what they call the most tyrannical reign they have ever experienced. They have tore the place to-" The man paused the news clip and stared at Thomas, scanning his face again. "Everyone thinks it was all the locals, that I do commend you for. The only people who know they had a helping hand is the locals themselves and they don't even know how it happened. They just saw an opportunity and took it. That I commend you for, you maintained stealth." The man smiled at Thomas, giving him a false sense of security and putting him at ease. "However, the rest is atrocious! If my men are correct you've already lost one of the five we authorised-"

"Hopefully he's alive we know his location! That's why we need the extra money, to mount a rescue mission." Thomas exasperatedly exclaimed. "Whatever, beyond that my sources stay that Salim is still alive you didn't even get the leader!" Thomas opened his mouth to protest but then firmly planted it shut. Confusion claimed him, Bird had definitely killed a man who said he was Salim. Bird had made that much clear, she had explained in great detail to Thomas.

"What?" Thomas eventually managed to choke out. The man shook his head and pressed the remote once more. Sputtering into life, the TV displayed a man that looked practically albino. He had a long blonde beard and long shaggy platinum hair. The only part of him that wasn't pale white were his eyes, which burned a bright hazel.

Thomas regarded the image and swore to himself internally, they'd been had. The 'Salim' his team had killed was most likely just a distraction to give the real Mr Alquedah time to escape. Spotting Thomas's obvious annoyance at the image, the man scoffed and began to play the video. "Yesterday a group of five people took my compound and killed countless men in their sleep. This dishonourable crew believes they caught and killed me in a crusade for 'justice.' If that team is listening out there keep this in mind, we have one of yours now." Salim span the camera around and revealed a photograph of a badly beaten Hush. "The truth is, the game was rigged from the start. I was never at that compound. You boys and girls just gave me time to get my plan into action. Soon will the day come when society falls and all the little soft piggies will squeal." The video cut out and left the two men in silence. Despite his extremism, Thomas could see why people followed Salim. He radiated charisma, practically oozed it. Mix that in with his perfect English (and no doubt perfect Arabic) and you'd have a very dangerous person indeed.

"It's bloody lucky we managed to intercept that. It was headed to every news network in Britain and all but said your names. It bloody showed an image of one of your team! Do you have any idea what kind of a security risk that is?" The man shouted, remaining sitting. His fat figure was no longer comedic, instead it took on a threatening form as Thomas was reprimanded. Being slapped with his failure, Thomas's confidence dissolved and he returned back to the quiet wiry young adult he usually was. "So to answer your question Mr Stevens, no you can't have more money from us. In fact the contract is dissolved, no more money, no more help. Furthermore, if you do another mission anything that would be illegal for a civilian will become illegal for you. The government no longer recognises your rinky dink operation."

"But they have chemical weapons. They tried to get me with one last night." Thomas tried to meagrely interject.

"Then hire more security. Maybe the five imbeciles you hired could be your body guards or something?" Mr Agemmeon laughed a cruel laugh, his demeanour completely changed from when Thomas first entered the room. "Give me your key-card and kindly get the hell out of my office. The repossession people will be there to collect your guns and illegals two days from now."

Forlorn, Thomas handed over his card and walked out the office raising his middle finger over his shoulder in a rare display of impoliteness. Once in the lobby again, the receptionist glared at Thomas and the atmosphere as a whole became unwelcoming. Taking the hint, he rushed out as fast as possible and leaped into the HummVee. The team tried to ask how things went but swiftly stopped when they saw his expression. "Tomorrow, ladies and gentleman we rescue Hush. Then we are moving our base of operations. I'm sick of this bloody country." The group resolved themselves and nodded. Curiosity gnawed at everyone's minds but they were united in their need to rescue one of their own and therefore stayed silent. The only ones showing any signs of dissent were Zeus and Nitro, who glared at each other childishly. Wrapped up in his own mental evaluation following his reprimand, Thomas didn't spot the tension and failed to reprimand them for it, so the pair stayed glaring at each other. They stayed glaring for the entire drive back to the training facility, much to Bird and Maple's immense disappointment.

Chapter Twenty

Everyone stood huddled back in Thomas's office as they had been when they were told off for the first time. Due to the lack of Hush, formality had gone out of the window and Thomas's obvious anxiety didn't help encourage the group. Following a long silence, he cleared his throat and did an admirable job to avoid eye contact. His eyes scanned over his desk, the ceiling and even a particularly interesting speck of dust on his desk. Once this strange dance was completed, he turned his probing gaze onto his finger-nails and began to speak. "We can't legally rescue Hush, our investors pulled out in lieu of the shambles that was your assault on the compound." Outrage burned brightly across everyone's face as they processed the information. "We did everything perfect, what more do they want?" Maple exploded, pounding the shield that hung limply at her side. "Some us could have tried little harder, I think." Nitro muttered under his breath, staring cuttingly at Zeus. For the first time since they had reunited, Thomas noticed the re-festering wound that was Nitro and Zeus's relationship. "I was shot, I actually put effort in what did you do? You failed to stop that one putting a bullet in Salim!" Zeus shouted, pointing towards Bird but mentally wounding Nitro in the process. Sensing an oncoming brawl, Thomas leapt in and silenced the two squabbling children. "Salim certainly doesn't have a bullet in him. Our investor showed me a clip were he was most definitely alive."

"But- but- I shot him." Bird stammered, French accent in full swing as her true emotion burst forth through the thin veneer of repression. "You shot someone Bird, and for that I am sorry it must have brought up some traumatic memories." Bird nodded as images of the greasy club owner falling to the floor, lifeless, flashed through her mind. The images had burnt themselves into her brain as permanent fixtures, dimming her thoughts. Swallowing, Bird refocused and dragged her memories from the pit that was the London Casino. "It did. Who did I-" She gulped again. "-kill then?"

"Probably one of Salim's lackeys." Maple said, turning to Thomas for confirmation. Thomas nodded and poured himself a drink from a compartment tucked into his desk. After taking a long, thoughtful, swig he sighed and began to talk once more. "The real Salim is alive, and we played right into his sick little plan. Our investors caught wind of this lapse and yanked our permissions and royalties. Roughly two days from now, a team of men will be here to collect our now illegal weapons and other contraband." Thomas took another deep drink and thought for a moment. "Everything we have done up until this point will be excused as we were operating under permissions granted to us."

"Why do I sense a however?" Maple jested, turning to Bird with a laugh. Bird did nothing but stare back with tears in her young eyes, so Maple quenched her laughter and turned her attention back to the increasingly tipsy Thomas. "However- anything we do from now on will be prosecuted." Thomas grabbed the bottle from underneath his desk and finished it off, pushing the glass away. Once he was done he poorly suppressed a belch and threw the bottle back into his desk. "So ladies and gentleman we are going to be as quick as possible with this." Everyone's hopes rose again and they released as powerful a cheer as they could manage with their lack of sleep. "Okay ladies and gentleman -*hic*- excuse me. Okay ladies and gentleman get some sleep you all clearly need it. We will be rolling out at eleven AM so that gives you-" with another hiccup he checked his watch, fumbling to focus on the timepiece's face. "-nine hours of sleep. That's quite good isn't it?" He giggled and gestured for everyone to leave. Saving him from embarrassing himself any further, three of them obliged and shuffled out of the tent.

The only one who remained was Nitro who, after receiving an incredibly dirty glare from Zeus, turned his attention back onto Thomas who was now playing with his empty glass. The bespectacled rich boy, rolled the glass back and forth across the desk, giggling, clearly unable to hold his liquor. Snapping his fingers, Nitro forced the child to focus on hm. "Why -hic- Why are you still here? Piss off." Thomas giggled. Firmly grasping the syringe, Nitro extracted it from his pocket. "You mention earlier that Salim possibly make chemical weapon yes?" Upon the mention of the mission and the sight of the syringe, Thomas instantly regained his focus. Any signs of girly gigglyness evaporated from his countenance and he gave an excellent appearance of being sober. "Where did you get that? -hic-" Thomas said, gesturing to the needle with great concern. "One of the terrorist had it at your house. I think maybe they try use it on you, yes?"
"Okay?" Thomas probed further, stifling another hiccup.
"I got terrorist with some of it, he went crazy! Had to put him down like rabid animal. Could maybe you analyse it see what is whilst we get Hush tomorrow?" Thomas nodded carefully, and then retrieved the syringe from Nitro's grip. Handling the syringe like it was a priceless glass statue, not a hint of shakiness in his grip, Thomas lowered it into his desk and sighed. With the syringe safely secured, Thomas's startling appearance of sobriety disappeared and he returned to giggling like a child. Nitro shuffled out of the tent leaving Thomas to attempt to glean information from his fingernails. Curiosity clouded Nitro's thoughts and his thought process was being especially slow. He was still mentally hesitant to attempt to lead, every time he had he hadn't had strong enough presence. In the hopes that after it was sorted his mind would clear and he could unravel the mystery, Nitro resolved to focus on his leadership in particular with this next mission.

Creeping into the sleeping quarters, Nitro spotted that everyone was fast asleep in their cots. They were held by firmly by the grips of nightmare ridden slumber and they all tossed and turned, still asleep. The only exception was Zeus who lay clutching his wound, fast asleep but smothered by pain nonetheless. Taking all of this in, Nitro crept over to his own cot and sank into it ready to enter his own realm of nightmares.

Chapter Twenty-One

Despite their lack of obligation to, everyone awoke four hours before they needed to leave. Feeling energised from the mere five hours of sleep, they all convened in the now empty warehouse that used to contain the mock-up embassy they had trained in all that time ago. Thomas had deposited a small fold-out table in the centre of the room for them to use then quickly vacated the building clutching his head. Gathered around the table, the group of four stared despairingly at the tablet Thomas had returned. The car that had taken Hush was parked in the middle of an industrial estate, outside a warehouse. This warehouse was much like the one they were currently stood in, (except a lot less high tech of course) in any other situation this would have been beneficial but because of the modular features of the warehouse the interior layout could quite literally be anything. The team couldn't plan for what amounted to ten's of thousands of possible interior layouts so they just stood staring at the exterior of the building through Nitro's tablet.

"I could go onto the roof? See if I can see anything through the sheet metal?" Zeus suggested.

"That is excellent idea." Nitro said in an attempt at leadership. Zeus shot him a dirty look, but didn't say anything insulting. "I could use my drones?" Bird suggested meekly.

"I don't know how we are going to do this, it seems impossible." Maple said, scratching her head with one hand still clutching her shield with the other.

"That not particularly helpful Maple, please bring good plan to table or don't say anything at all." Nitro assertively declared. Recognising immediately that the condescending tone wasn't the most effective way too lead this particular group, Nitro attempted to back-pedal with an apologetic smile plastered across his face. "I sorry Maple, I stressed is all. I say we go with Bird's idea. We need intel, she can get intel."

"Especially in conjunction with me on the roof." Zeus piped in with a scowl, keen for his plan to go ahead. "Especially with Zeus on roof." Nitro said to the utter surprise of Zeus. "We need to do this quickly. Everything we do will be illegal, get Hush leave no evidence, then leave. That the plan." Nitro announced confidently, signature smile finally returning after a night's sleep. Everyone nodded, pleased with the compromise and clear leader and traipsed outside. Once they were in the brisk air, they rushed over to the HummVee they had arrived in the night before and bustled in. Thankfully, due to a healthy dose of foresight, Thomas had left the keys in the ignition for them.

Touching his ear-piece, Nitro was glad to hear it connect to Thomas. "Hello?" Thomas asked, tinny through the small speaker. "Hello, Nitro reporting. We going early. Are we a go on operation stealth for stealth?" Thomas didn't respond for a moment as he thought through the planning. After a long pause he exclaimed. "Wait! Did you stock up on ammunition?" Thinking to himself Nitro swore and exited the jeep, sprinting towards the armoury. Extrapolating an answer from Nitro's silence, Thomas chuckled. "Once you've got the ammunition necessary you are clear to go. Remember be-"

"Quick and Quiet." Nitro finished Thomas's sentence and shut off the communications channel. Now in the scarily unguarded armoury, Nitro threw as many bullets as humanly possible into three duffel bags. The fourth one he filled with grenades of every type and shape. With his resupply complete, he heaved all four duffels upwards and sprinted back to the HummVee.

*   *   *

Bird had attempted to drone out the unassuming warehouse with little luck. There were no gaps in the walls and no-one opened a door. If anyone were to view the warehouse from a distance, as the group were, they could easily be fooled into believing the warehouse was empty. In fact the opposite was true, inside that warehouse possibly lay the hub for a terrorist organisation.

As the group surveyed the building they saw Zeus pop up from the roof like a mole exiting a hole. In a series of wild and barely decipherable gestures he indicated that inside the warehouse there was no traps, over one hundred terrorists and one object that could possibly be a bomb. Zeus then spoke into everyone else's ears via his ear-piece. "I'm unsure whether it's a bomb or not but there's something big and electrical in there." At hearing this Maple burst out laughing. Nitro and Bird turned an inquisitive eye onto her and raised their eyebrows, asking what was so funny without saying a word. "If he could use the ear-piece the whole time why did he bother with the millions of hand signals?" Maple explained through quiet laughter. Bird clocked onto the silliness first and burst out laughing herself. Engrossed in the mirth, Nitro joined in a brilliant smile blazing on his face whilst Zeus grimaced at them from the roof-tops.

"We have no option but to go in guns-blazing do we?" Maple asked once she had controlled her laughter, turning the mood back to seriousness. "No we don't. We have to go in blind, unfortunately." Nitro said. He then proceeded to turn to Bird. "If you want not go, that's okay. Leave now." Bird stood quietly for a moment, a tumultuous storm of emotion raging on her face. Once the storm had passed, a calm serendipity settled onto her face. "I'll do it. I tried to repress everything, that didn't work. So I'm going to go in there with you guys and allow myself to feel every emotion. I'm not going to allow myself to be consumed by it but I'm going to find a balance. For my sake and for Hush's. Not that I like the guy that much." She laughed in an attempt to lighten the mood. "I know I am capable of succeeding in this mission and coping with it

emotionally. I just need to prove that to you guys and myself."
Maple smiled emotionally at hearing her old mentality echoed
back at her. After hearing it from Bird she couldn't help but
wonder if she had it wrong all along. She didn't know she
could handle it before, that's why she was so desperate to prove
herself. It was plain old insecurity blanketed under a rug of
faux confidence. Hearing Bird begin to adopt a healthier
version of Maple's original thought process ended Maple's
identity crisis and she resolved that she wouldn't bother about
proving herself. Instead she'd focus on what she was good at,
her job. Not pleasing others and reaching their expectations,
the only expectations she'd exceed would be her own. To hell
with the judgemental people she used to fear.

Nitro smiled wider seeing the grins of acceptance spreading
across the girls' faces. He liked to think that under his careful
guidance this shattered vase of a team was now re-gluing itself
back together. Zeus still scowled from the roof-tops like some
miserable vigilante but Nitro returned him a smile. Yes, the
man's childishness endlessly irked him but with a little bit of
encouragement, Nitro was sure that him and Zeus could
become uneasy friends. Not the sort of friends that would
invite each other to their weddings, but the sort of friends that
you would invite to get blind drunk with if no-one else
presented themselves.

Epiphany's and the beginnings of further character growth
achieved, the three of them situated themselves in front of the
warehouse's side entrance whilst Zeus settled in on the roof to
provide cover. Nitro heaved a charge out of his pack and
unfurled it onto the door, he reasoned that it would be quicker
and easier than breaking down the door. Breaking down the
door would take time and alert the terrorists, whilst the charge
would be sudden and give the group the highly valued element
of surprise. Yanking the pin out of the charge, Nitro instructed
Maple to lead the charge with her shield once the door blew

away. She nodded and steeled herself. The *Thunk Thunk Thunk* of the charge working its magic was putting her on edge in a strange way. It was a good sort of anxiety, an excited anticipation to rescue a team-member that had given her friend trouble. Bird stood poised over Maple's shoulder tightly gripping her desert eagle. She was ready to take another life, but finally ready to deal with the consequences of such an action. Nitro was holding his breath, smile still on his face. The smile didn't quite reach his eyes however. Now that there was slightly less friction between the team he could focus on the syringe and he didn't like any of the conclusions. With a mental wave of the hand, he pushed all thoughts aside and focused on the upcoming challenge. If he didn't properly lead this mission everyone would likely die. They had no idea what the interior looked like and they had no plans beyond, rush in there, kill everyone, except Hush, and get out.

If Zeus was right and there was an explosive or other electronic device that needed to be diffused, then that would be a whole other challenge. Switching mental gears to focus on the now instead of the soon, Nitro counted down the seconds until the charge fully detonated.

once again unto the breach
OPERATION STEALTH FOR STEALTH

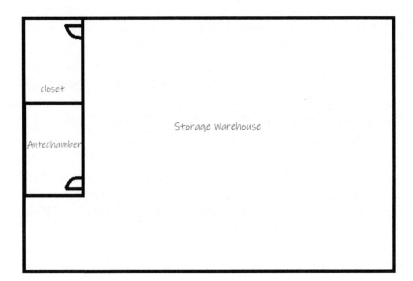

"Only those who risk going too far can possibly find out how far one can go."

Chapter Twenty-Two

With a mighty roar, the charge detonated and reduced the flimsy door to matchsticks. The gates to hell now open, the team of three rushed in with a perpetually sulking guardian angel keeping watch overhead. "There are three men through the door. Shall I handle them for you? I know you struggle sometimes" The guardian angel asked, muttering the last bit under his breath with a cruel chuckle. "No, it time we proved we worth it." Nitro replied, glancing at the women. One with cutting emeralds gleaming out of her head and one with blazing diamonds. Seeing the confidence from the two girls, Nitro smiled and shut off the communication channel with Zeus. The smoke cleared and revealed the three men stood menacingly. Seemingly unfazed by the magnesium burn that had recently emanated from Nitro's charge, they threw themselves into action, taking fighting stances and radiating aggression. The team fell utterly silent as they were bogged down by confusion. They should've had the upper hand here, why didn't they?

Seeing the opportunity lying beneath the moment of stupefied silence, one charged directly at Maple. As he got closer she came face to face with herself. The terrorists were wearing reflective foil over riot helmets. Not only did this give them the uncanny appearance of some fifties vision of alien life, but it also presumably protected them from bright lights. Meaning flash-bangs would effectively be useless.

Still charging, the central terrorist stampeded into Maple. Jolted, everyone fell out from behind Maple's weighty shield and had to quickly readjust as a single terrorist engaged each of them one on one. Maple's adversary yanked a blade out of his belt and flipped it between his grip, indicating Maple should advance. Impressed with the clearly well trained, callow, confidence Maple did exactly that. She shoved forward, activating the freezing water jets in the process. For a hollow moment the water looked like it was slowing down the terrorist. However, after he had evaluated what was happening to him he continued his crusade with as much vigour as ever. He pummelled through the hydro-attack as if there was nothing at all in his way. After a few seconds that crystallised into years for Maple, his groping blade reached her shield. In the battle between the tough polymers of Maple's shield and her assailant's knife, Maple would have assumed her shield would have won. However the opposite was true. With a horrendous, scraping racket, the knife cut a thin gouge through Maple's shield. In amazement, Maple stared at the tip of the knife poking through her shield. With her confidence shaken, she barrelled backwards almost falling over in the process. In a magnificent stroke of luck the sudden movement took her assailant by surprise and disarmed him. The knife was still poking through the slender slice in the shield and the terrorist looked at his now empty hands with a quiet *huh?*

Now re-armed with the upper hand, Maple shook the knife loose from her shield and directed the water jets directly onto the previously mentioned shield. Freezing instantly, the water turned the shield into one sheet of ice. If the assailant cracked or shattered this sheen it would be immediately replaced with a fresh coat. Unfortunately, shaking the knife loose had placed the blade back into the terrorist's grasp and he lunged for it hungrily. He slickly flipped the knife in his grip once more and rolled his shoulders, gesturing once more for Maple to advance. The canary eating grin that was surely on his face beneath the ridiculous riot helmet shot a flash of rage through Maple and she obliged his cocky request.

The noise that echoed this time as blade collided with shield was less cringe worthy and more awe inspiring. With a mighty *shwing* like a samurai sword being drawn, the blade bounced harmlessly off of the frozen surface. Staring at the terrorist through her shield, Maple took her moment to take on the air of a canary stuffed cat and relished every petty second of it. Incensed by her small victory, she pushed forwards once again. Wielding the shield as one might wield a folding chair in a cartoonish martial arts fight, Maple engaged the terrorist. The battle of ice on blade was practically biblical. Maple would hit the terrorist a few times and then he'd hit her back. The blade broke through the ice and pierced the shield a couple of spine chilling times. Once it even made contact with her skin and cut an embarrassingly shallow wound. It bled a microscopic amount and then scabbed within seconds. Maple's terror was replaced by an irresistible urge to laugh as she realised how minor he had managed to injure her whilst giving it his all. Laughing in his face, Maple shoved the man backwards with her shield and swept his legs whilst he stumbled. He fell onto his backside, dazed. Planting her boot firmly on his chest, Maple pushed him flat to the floor. As he strained in a desperate attempt to escape, he revealed his neck from under the helmet and Maple slammed her shield down on it. With a squelching crunch the shield connected, not decapitating him but certainly robbing him of his life. The shielding left it's indent on the man's exposed neck, as tires leave tracks on road-kill and Maple had to look away. The viscera was shocking, even for someone as experienced as her. Job done, she glanced around and drank in the other two's fights.

Nitro was locked in a fist-fight, throwing slug after slug. His terrorist returned the favour and just when it looked like Nitro was about to lose the bludgeoning match; he wrenched the silly reflective helmet off of the terrorist's head. Now exposing the balaclava smothered head of the terrorist, he threw a mean right hook and connected with a *crack*. Just like that, the terrorist's lights went out and he crumbled to the floor. Nitro made eye contact with Maple shooting her a grin. After a jaunty moment his eye line slide over Maple's shoulder and onto Bird. Eye's growing wide, he gestured for Maple to look at Bird.

Some of her movements were clumsy and untrained still but she dodged every slash of the blade smoothly. She was oil sliding across water and she was ready for his every move. Without her anxiety bogging her down, Bird could tap into her deep routed knack for combat. In a few impressive flashes of movement, Bird knocked the terrorists down to his knees and drew her gun. Surprisingly, she flashed him an apologetic smile and swung her gun around. Now that the barrel was no longer pointing at the terrorist, Bird allowed the poor bastard a few moments of confusion before striking him across the face with the weapon's stocky grip. The impact broke his nose, opened a gouge on his lip and cheek and knocked him out, but it was non-lethal. Bird felt swelling pride as she turned around and saw smiles of joy beaming from Nitro and Maple. She had avoided marring her soul with further death. Sure, the sight of blood still made her feel queasy but she had learned to handle death and injury healthily for someone in her line of work.

Chapter twenty-three

Now that the pressing matter of the terrorists were handled, the team had time to inhale there environment. They were stood in a small room about six by six metres. The walls seemed to be fashioned from some sort of lightweight polymers, presumably so they could be moved upon the tenants whims. A coppery, tangy, scent hung in the air. It didn't smell bad, just wrong. If the compound emanated an air of death, this warehouse reeked of conniving treachery.

Nitro asked Zeus for a report and was surprised to hear that Zeus had taken out four men in the room beyond. This information was troubling however, as it meant the people beyond the door were surely waiting for the team in the inner sanctum of the warehouse, teeth bared and gun's cocked.

Baring this information in mind, Nitro kicked the bottom of the door in. The cheap wood splintered and left a small hole. Maple stared at this seemingly random outburst in confusion but Bird understood immediately. Unholstering her drone, Bird donned the glasses controls and smiled at Nitro. He returned the grin and gestured for her to go ahead.

With a flourish, Bird activated the small drone and began to pilot it. Driving it through the hole in the door, she was perplexed to find no one waiting on the other side. However the most interesting part is that beyond the door laid a regular warehouse. Countless shelves lined the walls and towered high, huge monoliths casting their shadows down upon the exposed concrete floor. Amazed, Bird piloted the drone to the top of the roof and purveyed all. In-between the shelving units were the slumped silhouettes of the men Zeus had taken out. With a gasp Bird realised that countless of these silhouettes littered the aisles between the shelving units. At first she thought Zeus had been busier than he let on, but then as she piloted the drone closer to one of these mystery bodies the truth became clear.

Every single terrorist in the warehouse had killed themselves.

Bird relayed the information to a shocked Maple and Nitro. Nitro then passed the information along to Zeus who, after a torrent of ill mannered jokes and insults on Nitro's behalf, mumbled something about that making sense.
With everyone fully informed, Bird turned her attention back to her little drone. As she pushed forwards through the warehouse she found more and more terrorists dead in the aisles.
Following an eternity of repeating rows of shelves and death, she saw a small door tucked away to the side and then immediately forgot. Bird's attention was stolen as she spotted the 'bomb' that Zeus had seen. It wasn't a bomb by any account. Instead it was a large obelisk with the same fluid Nitro had seen in the syringe rushing around it. The magenta fluid pulsed around tubes and wires like it was a living thing. The obelisk was the sort of futuristic high-tech naff that Bird expected Thomas to have, not the sort of stuff that terrorists could have. On top of the pillar was a nozzle that currently was clamped shut and at the bottom was a keyboard with a living man clattering away at it. Bird couldn't determine whether the strange object was a missile or what so she silently showed the rest of the group the image. After a slack-jawed silence, Nitro informed Zeus who surprisingly didn't reply.

Up there on the roof, Zeus had located the small side room of his own accord. He used a furious cocktail of the sensors on his sniper, shooting holes to peep through and random guesswork but eventually he located it. Pulling a breaching charge out of his bag that he had 'borrowed' from Nitro, Zeus planted it on the roof and waited for his time. Using the thermal scope, he could see extra heat in the room indicating the presence of about three to four people. However for whatever reason the roof was slightly too thick in that particular spot and he couldn't line up a proper shot. Especially if his gut feeling was correct. Zeus's gut was telling him that if Hush was anywhere in the warehouse he would be locked away in this small side room and he didn't want to blindly fire into the room, just in case he was correct in his belief. So instead he waited, waited to see what would happen with the rest of the team. If they didn't need assistance Zeus would manually light the charge and go in guns blazing.

Back in the warehouse, the team had eased the door open to the suicide and shelves room. Slowly pushing their way to the back of the warehouse where they knew the contraption lay they winded in-between everything. As they got closer and closer to the contraption the team could hear a hum. A strange mechanical hum that buzzed and changed rhythm almost as much as an orchestra changes instrument. Conducting this chorus of death was the man who Bird had seen. The *tippity tap* of his keyboard added to the machine's hum in an overwhelming cacophony.

Trying her best to ignore the lifeless corpses at her feet, Bird lead the charge. Since she was the one that knew the way Bird reached the man first. Before she could shout out to question the man's motives however he span on the balls of his feet and faced them. Taken aback, Bird took an involuntary step backwards and ended up inline with the rest of the group. "You're late." The man said with a smile. "Hello, I'm Salim Alquedah and you must be the little piggies sent to rescue your feisty friend."

"What have you done with him?" Maple shouted, slightly adjusting her shield so that it protected Bird's legs. Salim spotted the small movement with a smug smirk and completely disregarded Maple's question. "You realise you fell right for the bait again right?" Salim laughed emotionlessly. "I keep getting you little pigs to squeal on my command." He then proceeded to imitate a pig squealing, the cruel noise bouncing off the walls of the warehouse. "Bait?" Bird asked, slowly piloting the drone over the contraption as best she could without getting caught. "You'll see soon enough, You certainly will. I'm not willing to answer any questions, you won't be able to torture information out of me. The truth is, my dearest pigs, the game was rigged from the start." With that cryptic remark, the real Salim span around and slapped a key on his keyboard. A warning light they didn't even notice was on switched to green, bathing Salim in the sickly hue of green and magenta as he turned back around. With a strange mischievous smirk Salim started to reach behind his back.

Assuming the worst of the worst, Bird rose her gun at the nods of her comrades. "May God forgive me." She muttered under her breath in French.

She pulled the trigger.

The trigger pulled back the firing pin.

The firing pin collided with the bullet's primer

.

The primer ignited the bullet's gunpowder.

The expanding gases from the resulting explosion pushed the bullet out of the barrel at four-hundred and seventy metres a second.

This angel of a bullet then continued on its final ride, slicing through air, too fast for a human eye to see. With a satisfying *thunk* it reached its final destination. The bullet ripped through the oddly smug Salim's face and out the back. The exiting bullet took most of the delusional man's brain with it leaving a smear of gooey gray on the still glowing cylinder. Bird lowered the smoking gun, gripped in the claws of acceptance. She was a sinner. She had let killing corrupt her soul, even if there was no God she would have to live with her actions for the rest of her life. Bird knew that pulling the trigger whilst in this state of mind would mean that she would forever see the bullet slamming its way through the terrorist leaders head, but she had done it anyway because it was the right thing to do. Nitro smiled a pitying smile and Maple stroked Bird lovingly on the back. The small gestures helped a surprising amount and just as she was starting to reach a state of Zen two gunshot's echoed behind them. "Catching up to friends I assume." Nitro said, glancing back in reference to the two that they had left unconscious on entry. Looking at the corpses that littered the aisles, placing the metallic sting of blood in the air Maple couldn't help but agree.

"OK ladies, something fishy here. I think we may not be done. Bird kindly activate your drone's defuser technology. Probably not do anything but worth a shot. Maple, I want you to stay with me and investigate this strange thing." Nitro said, taking charge for once. "Bird go look for Hush. I think he here, I got a feeling about it you know? I inform Zeus about what happening now, yes." Now done with his instructions, he trusted the girls to get on with it as he fiddled with his ear-piece.

Chapter twenty-four

Maple busied herself on the strange machine's keyboard whilst Bird engaged the drone to begin its defuser mode. Once the mode was engaged an impossibly long loading bar popped up and Bird sighed. Seeing Maple struggling with the computer systems, Bird rushed over and gave her some pointers as well as an encouraging smile. At first it seemed odd that Nitro had tagged Maple with the computing task, but now Bird saw it for what it truly was; an opportunity to share knowledge and work better together.

With Maple sufficiently helped, Bird left her in the care of Nitro and jogged in the rough direction of the door she had seen.

Nitro finally got in contact with Zeus and informed him that everything so far with any luck was a-okay. Zeus replied the affirmative but followed it with a quiet obligatory insult. He was clearly distracted by something and his heart wasn't really in it. Nitro chuckled, disconnected the line and turned to Maple to help her with the investigation of the obelisk.

On the roof, Zeus activated the breaching charge and shimmied backwards away from it. It began its menacing detonation and Zeus felt a smile gracing his lips. He was once again thinking how stupid the arguing was and realising how childish he was being. As the charge ticked down he laughed at how he'd been squabbling with Nitro like a child and resolved to actually fix their relationship properly after this Misson.

*   *   *

Hush, tied to a chair and unable to move as pain pulsed from his badly healed bullet wound, spat the blood out of his mouth at the feet of the sick man that had been torturing him. This act was such a ritual at this point that the torturer and his two body guards laughed. "Not much good that's going to do is it? Now please tell me. Who do you work for? Is it Thomas Stevens?" The torturer strolled over to the small metal table that held all of his 'instruments' and idly stroked the pliers.

"Who the 'ell is Thomas Stevens?" Hush spat through multiple missing teeth that the torturer had removed. "I 'aint nothing but a merc. Some fellas in balaclava's hired me. I just took the bloody money I didn't ask their pissing address!" The torturer stopped fingering his 'instruments' and cocked his head curiously.

"You know we don't take to lying too kindly." He said, backed up by the cruel laughter of his body-guards. "I'll ask you this one time now. I want the truth." The torturer said, grasping something tightly behind his back. "Are you the operator known as Hush, hired by Thomas Steven's and funded by a governmental committee?" Shocked at the intense breadth of knowledge the torturer possessed, Hush stayed silent momentarily. "Well?"

"For fuck sake I bloody told 'ya I haven't the faintest who the hell this Thomas bloke is!" The torturer looked like he believed Hush momentarily before a grin broke his facade. He drew the thing he was gripping behind his back out and allowed the light to glint off of it. It was a rather beat up spoon. Gulping, Hush stared the man directly in the eye. "Who the 'ell is Hush. I'm James Daniel." The man approached wielding the spoon with immense gravitas, as if it were a mighty sword. "Woah. Come on lad you don't have to do this you can-" Hush stopped speaking as soon as he realised it wouldn't have any effect at all.

The spoon plunged deep into the corners of his left eye in a supernova of pain and just as the terrorist was about to start leveraging it, the room exploded in a flash of white. A shard of pain exploded through Hush and as his vision readjusted he realised he now only had one half of his vision. The torturer had taken a panicked step back whilst blinded and held onto the spoon as he did it. The sudden movement had yanked Hush's left eye out of it's socket, cleanly. The poor appendage now lay on the battered spoon, resting on the ground where the torturer had dropped it. Hush didn't feel too much pain just yet, but he knew that was just the adrenaline and shock cocktail his brain had coursing through his body. In half an hour he would feel the lack of the eye immensely. He most likely would be immobilised with agony, if the torturer didn't decide to just up and kill him.

Now recovered, the torturer lunged for his pliers but was stopped by the room, once again, blossoming in a brilliant white accompanied by a shrill whistling noise as his ears reeled from the explosion. Hush felt chunks of drywall rain down upon him and he looked up to see Zeus dropping in from the ceiling like a guardian angel. Zeus shot the body guards on entry, but didn't spot the torturer stumbling around still blind. Zeus started to work on the ropes that held Hush, barely even blinking at the state Hush was in.

Just as Zeus was halfway through the ropes, the small room burst into a flurry of action once more. The torturer's groping fingers found a gun. He yanked the gun upwards aiming at Hush and just as he was about to pull the trigger, the door behind him flew open. Spinning around in surprise, his grip on the gun shifted a little and he came face to face with Bird.

Bang!

Bang!

Two shots echoed and were silenced by the room's soundproofing. The torturer fell to the floor and Bird turned to Hush and Zeus with a smile. Hush returned the smile with a blasé smoulder, ignoring his horrendous state but Zeus didn't do anything. Instead he clutched his neck, stumbled backward a few steps, forwards a few and then crumpled to the floor. He choked out a "tell Nitro I'm sorry for being a dick." in a gurgled bloody breath. By the time Bird slammed down onto her knees next to Zeus the life had clearly exited him and he lay there, wide eyed with a laugh dead on his lips.

Turning to Hush for consolation, Bird instead found more horror. Tears in her eyes and a scream she would never express stored in her throat, she really took in Hush. His entire face was soaked in blood. Along his face were rows and rows of incredibly thin, yet deep, cuts. With a mouth full of more empty gum than teeth he had the appearance of some demon. Raking her eyes upwards across his face she spotted the missing eye with a small yelp blood seeped out of the empty socket, soaking his shirt. He looked like he had single handedly fought every demon in hell, never-mind looking like a demon. After a few minutes of horrified silence, Bird stumbled to her feet and made her way over to Hush. She finished cutting his ropes and as soon as he was free he gripped her in a tight bear-hug, soaking her in his blood. "Bloody 'ell I'm sorry. You're gonna be okay. You got that? You are." Hush released Bird and did his best job to saunter to the door. "Now if you don't mind I need a lash and a good doc'." He said, weakly chuckling and exiting.

After he was gone, Bird crawled over to Zeus and cradled his sniper rifle. It seems strange but it was all she could think of doing, it was the best thing that represented his legacy. His corpse was an insult to who he had tried to be. His rifle was more apt. She stayed there for a long, long, time. She didn't like the man much but she laid there crying nonetheless. Once she was done she heaved herself onto her feet, his rifle over her shoulder, and walked back into the main room.

When Bird got back to where the obelisk was she was utterly surprised by the lack of obelisk. Instead of a strange contraption, there was a large empty space and a gigantic uneven hole in the roof. Standing around this empty space was a devastated Nitro and Maple. Maple sat on her shield whilst Nitro fiddled with his hands. There wasn't the faintest of smiles on his face. For the first time since any of the girls had known him, his face was entirely contorted into a sullen look of despair. "Hi." Bird managed to timidly choke.

"Hush told us." Nitro said. Beyond that the other two didn't say anything in reference to Zeus, instead they glanced at the rifle on Bird's shoulder, suppressed a sob and changed the subject entirely. "The thing, it uh- it took flight like a missile and left." Maple said, voice cracking with a mixture of devastation for Zeus and confusion at the device. "Hush went get ambulance. Everyone's sorted best possible for the situation. We go leave now, go to Thomas. I already informed him on tonight's tragedy. He waiting with debriefing. Nothing we can do now." Nitro said. His mournful tone was dismally bleak and the two women didn't argue.

Everyone was submerged in the same tar pit of grief. Fighting to not let it consume them, they all piled back into the HummVee and made the long journey back.

By now the day was deep in the throes of night and they all stared out at the glittering lights of the industrial district as they drove through it. Every sparkle that glittered felt like a betrayal. Every glittering light was one light burning brightly when Zeus should be instead. No one in the car liked the man, but they could all sense that with a little bit of work he could have been better. Not to mention how good he was at what he did. Everyone reflected on their relationships with the now deceased Russian. Especially the permanently scarred Bird, who had came the closest to breaking in the way that turned Zeus into the man he was. Having come so close to that form of mental illness, she related in particular and ached at knowing how she could have helped him if he had just gotten out of there alive.

Debriefing
"Grief is in two parts, the first is loss. The second is remaking
of life."

Chapter twenty-five

The journey back from the warehouse was unsurprisingly more harrowing than the journey from Syria. Yes the team had 'succeeded' but at what cost. Hush was maimed, going to survive sure, but maimed. A strange missile had escaped their grasp and Zeus had died. To anyone else it would be seen as somewhat of a success, the leader and majority of a large terrorist organisation had been taken out, but to everyone on the team they had failed.

The loss would stay with them forever but everyone cheered up somewhat at seeing the training facility rise over the horizon. Hopefully this would be the last time they ever see the place that had started this mess. Sitting on an oil barrel outside Thomas's tent was Hush. He still looked awful but the colour was slowly returning to his face. Whatever the doctor had given him was clearly working a treat as he grinned smugly at the sight of the car approaching.

As everyone stepped out of the truck a silence crystallised for a few seconds as they stared down Hush. He seemed unfazed by the weary stares and kept offering a smirk. Slapped over his eye was a black eyepatch with the pattern of a gold vine running across it. It matched his knife and made Bird giggle slightly through the tears. "You look like a James Bond villain." she laughed, covering her mouth. "Wow 'ell of a way to say thanks for not revealing any information under torture." Hush said, stroking the knife on his belt. Even though his manner pointed towards him being fine mentally there was little signposts. Little mannerisms revealed that he was undergoing at least some form of mental battle. Those with a keen eye could notice that he never stopped touching his knife. He petted it like a dog and generally just kept a piece of the handle in his grip. Bird noticed this and chose to ignore it. Knowing Hush, he definitely didn't want to talk about it.

Nitro finally composed himself and walked over to Hush, clapping him on the back. "Good to see you." He exclaimed loudly, a beam lighting up Hush's beaten face. Despite his awful state, Hush somehow looked younger. It was like the mission had revitalised him in a way he'd been sorely needing for years.

Nitro began chattering idly to Hush in his still broken English and the girls took the opportunity to talk together once more. Taking a few strategic steps out of the men's earshot, they embraced. "How are you doing Bird?"

"The weight of all these deaths it's a lot. But I will be okay." Bird said, wiping a tear away.

"I know." Maple paused for a moment, taken deep in the throes of thought. "You know what I figured out recently? Why do we care about people's opinions? We only live once and if we take so many lives in our lifetime we sure as hell better live for ourselves."

"Do you not feel the pressure to make sure your worth it?"

"What do you mean?"

"I mean, do you ever feel like you need to be a certain amount of good to prove that you were the one that should have won the fight and not the other guy?"

Maple took in Bird with a sad smile. "Hey, I know it's pretty easy to fall into that thought process but its just survivors guilt. Don't let the dead slowly kill you. You're strong, clever, smart and intelligent. If you live for yourself you'll achieve amazing things. Don't live for the dead."

Realising that Maple was right, Bird swung Zeus's rifle from her shoulder and stared at it. The hunk of engineering radiated presence, like Zeus was still there. Bird ejected the magazine and realised she was being silly. Since she had picked up his rifle Bird had resolved to become a great sniper to honour him. Now she realised that the best way to honour him would be to great in her own right. From now on she would try to build a legacy on the foundation of Zeus. Maple patted Bird and the soldier and dragged her out of her thoughts. "Come on 'Canuck, we've got to go. Look." Placing the magazine back in the rifle with reverence, Bird turned. Sure enough, the boys had stopped chattering about whatever they were whittling away the time with and were now looking at them expectantly. The girls fell into step and then began the march into Thomas's tent, together. They were one unit, all in step, all equal. Everyone had a different smile lighting up their face. Bird: a smile of acceptance, she would honour Zeus in the best possible way. Maple: a smile of victory, Salim and his terrorist organisation was dead. Nitro: a beaming grin of victory and comradeship, the team were getting on. His only regret was that Zeus didn't have time to become a true part of the team once more. Finally, there was Hush who's smirk told a thousand stories. His cockiness had been replaced by faux cockiness in an effort for humour and his smirk said that he was proud. He would never put it into words but he was immensely proud at what the team had managed to accomplish, they had taken down a terrorist organisation and rescued him from the grips of a torturer. Sure they had suffered little losses all over the place: the loss of the obelisk/missile/whatever, the loss of his eye, the loss of Zeus. However, Hush didn't focus on that. In fact the main thing he was frustrated about is the fact that he didn't get to see the team in action more.

The four flung open Thomas's door and walked into a beaming Thomas. Thrusting a very expensive drink into each of their hands he began to chatter away. "Good to see you Hush."

"Good to see 'ya too skipper."

"Hopefully you'll be back on your feet soon enough."

"Aye, give me a couple of days and I'll be boxin' like a kangaroo. I sure will."

Thomas laughed and indicated for everyone to take a sip of their drink. Everyone did and even those that didn't like booze were pleasantly surprised. The drink wasn't very strong and had a hint of cherry and cinnamon that would hit the back of your throat and make you think of sweet things. "Sherry, I had them distill a slightly weaker variant so you could actually taste it." Thomas explained laughing haughtily.

"Not to bring down mood, but what about the government? Are they collecting everything tomorrow still?"

Thomas laughed even louder and indicated Nitro to take a swig of his drink. "That's the absolutely excellent bit, ladies and gentleman. The boss of the man I meet, the man who told me we were being shut down, he saw what you guys did." Thomas then placed his own drink down and broke into a short round of applause. "Bravo by the way." He picked up his drink again and finished the glass. "Anyway the big boss said we were excellent and possibly a useful asset if you were trained a tad more. He doubled our funding and reinstated our licence." Still beaming through his glasses, Thomas pulled out the sherry and refilled his glass. With a laugh he rose the glass and proposed a toast. "It's been tough but you ladies and gentleman have proved you are worth your salt. This is to you!" Everyone else raised their glass to match Thomas and took a victorious sip. The drinks burn felt like the side effect of a long fought battle finally won and for a moment everyone forgot about the escaped missile. Still engrossed in their glasses of ambrosia, the team watched as Thomas lowered his glass and laughed even more. "Also, word is that because you saved everyone's hide the government has dubbed you guys Operation Cavalry. I liked the name so I had these made." Thomas produced four strips of black fabric. 'Operation Cavalry' was embroidered onto the fabric in a red thread. "You just stick it too the velcro on your left shoulder." The team members took the fabric strips and attached them firmly to the velcro on their arms.

For a minute everyone stood still, silent, smiling and proud but then Nitro spoke up. "A strange thing it got away. Big glowing machine, you know what happen to it?" Nitro said placing his half finished drink back onto Thomas's desk. "Oh, don't worry about that. The government saw a strange object in their airspace, panicked and immediately blew it up with another missile." Thomas said, snickering with his mouth buried in his glass. "So they saw it and shat themselves basically." Hush said, chuckling. Once Hush started his rare chuckle everyone joined in, united by mirth for a few seconds. At the end they couldn't remind why they were laughing to begin with. Once the tears were wiped away, they turned back to the task at hand. "There was liquid in machine. Destroying the missile maybe rained that on people." Nitro said as his worry returned. Thomas cocked his head in curiosity, subtly telling Nitro to continue. "It look like same stuff that was in syringe I gave you." For a split almost imperceivable second Thomas's eyes narrowed but then they returned back to a state of mirth. "Don't worry Nitro, if there was a problem the government would have handled it. I'll finish the analysis on the syringe straight after this though, just in case."

An awkward silence began to form and Thomas shattered it with a laugh. "Look at all you. I'm so proud of you all." Thomas said, walking around his desk and over to them all. He hugged Bird. At first she tensed at the sudden advance and then realised it was a hug of pride and relaxed. Once he was done with Bird he moved onto maple, who ended up hugging him back tighter. Hush winced as he knew what was coming. The wiry tech nerd untangled himself from Maple and turned to him with a smile. "Piss right off, mate." Hush said as he stepped back. Thomas guffawed and ignored him, wrapping him in a tight hug. At first Hush hung limply but then he resolved to return the hug. The awkwardness radiated from Hush, almost painfully, as he patted Thomas on the back. Quietly chuckling, Thomas disengaged himself from Hush and turned to Nitro. Nitro smiled and wrapped Thomas in a bear hug. Beaming, the old friends embraced for a long time. It was only halted when Thomas softly pushed him away. "I wanted a hug not death by compression." He said, laughing.

With his gesture of goodwill complete Thomas addressed the group as a whole again. "If none of you guys want to quit right now, we can get you contracted up. You'll be paid a salary instead of by the job."

"How much is it?" Maple asked.

"Probably double minimum wage." Bird said, guessing.

"Quadruple. Quadruple minimum wage." Thomas said with a smirk. Silence fell as everyone's jaws collectively hit the floor. "You just got to sign these and Operation Cavalry will officially be formed." Thomas said as he produced four contracts from his desk with the flair of a magician. Scrabbling for pens, everyone grabbed a copy and quickly signed them.

With the legalities and talk complete, Thomas ushered them out into the night to get some rest. "You need some rest ladies and gentleman. Tomorrow you train. You need to be ready for anything." With that he retreated back into his office leaving them alone. The two ladies and two men stared at each other smiling. They had suffered failures together, they had achieved victory together and they would forge a new future together. Sure all of their small squabbles weren't resolved yet, but for the moment at least they were one unit. One body working perfectly in tandem, each operator a part of a machine. They continued grinning at each other, all of them bruised or bloody from their adventures so far. The Operation Cavalry patch burned brightly on their shoulders and they were prepared to make a name for themselves. Together they would tackle any problem and crush it to tiny bits of metaphorical, and possibly literal shrapnel, all as one unit. All as Operation Cavalry...

Epilogue
"Every experience, good or bad, you have to learn from."

Thomas stared at his desk. In front of him were two files. One red, one yellow. The red one was from his analysis department and the yellow from the government. Thomas had just finished reading both and was sat there utterly shell-shocked. The yellow folder documented a break out of rabies in a small town near the industrial district. This was significant as the town that the file mentioned was down wind of where the terrorist's strange missile was destroyed. According to the file, people's pulses were dropping impossibly low. Following this medical curio, the patient would foam at the mouth and exhibit all the standard symptoms of rabies. However, instead of irritability and irrationality which was the standard for rabies, these patients lost their minds entirely. Those who were infected would lose all rationality and act completely inhuman. They would babble nonsense, seemed immune to any sort of pain or injury unless completely fatal and would attempt to bite anything living.

The file then went on to chatter random legalese about how the government was employing a plan to keep this 'strange phenomenon' contained. Any man with any sort of sense could see that the plan was half-baked and insane, yet for some reason the government were going through with it. The plan was as follows: restrain the infected in hospitals and keep them there on painkillers until they inevitably died from the rabies. It wasn't a solution as much as it was an avoidance, but as long as the problem actually was rabies, the infected would die after a week or two.

Thomas then shifted his focus to the second folder. Inside the folder was the analysis of the contents of the syringe Nitro had brought him. At first the scientists had thought the curious liquid to be dilute liquefied uranium mixed with magenta dye, but on closer inspection under a microscope they discovered something else in there... Millions of instances of Lyssavirus, commonly known as the rabies virus. These viruses weren't the standard Lyssavirus however. These ones stayed alive in the uranium; heavily mutated but alive. Presumably the terrorists had selectively bred the virus to survive in high radiation environments and then allowed the radiation to mutate them until they got the one they wanted. This brand new, real nasty variant of rabies had a few tricks up it's sleeve. After lots of experimenting, the scientists determined that this variant not only didn't kill its host, but in fact took control of the host. Anyone infected with the virus would become a machine hell-bent on infecting more. They would lose their humanity to an incurable disease and keep powering forth, long after death should take a normal human. From what Thomas's scientists had found so far the infected weren't invincible, they just healed quicker as the virus hijacked their platelets and improved them. What really rubbed salt in the wound however, was the fact that just like normal rabies this virus was completely uncurable. The scientists had found that you could slow it down with antivirals, but once you'd been bitten you would be infected no matter what.

At the foot of the folder was a small note from one of the scientists saying that possibly under the right conditions the virus could be aerosolised.

Thomas stared weighty at one folder then the other and then back and so on. He continued this way for a while, contemplating. Even if the government had actually controlled the aerosol version as they claimed to have, there was no way in hell they'd manage to contain the bites. If Thomas's estimations were correct, the infection would take over eighty percent of the country in three months. Reaching into his desk, Thomas grabbed the forty year old whiskey he'd bought when he made his first million and an old revolver. Pouring a glass, he savoured the ambrosia and checked the gun. Once his glass was empty he placed the bottle carefully back in his desk and planted the barrel of the revolver in his mouth. Praying that the team would handle the infection, he pulled the trigger...

"In the end, we will not remember not the words of our enemies, but the silence of our friends."

Notes from the author

Thank you for reading my first novel. I personally don't think it's very good but thank you for taking a chance on it nonetheless. Ever since I was a young boy I've loved reading and have liked to think I'm a good writer. All throughout my childhood I tried my hand at writing stories, never quite starting or finishing them. The fact I have managed to finish this one novel at the age of fifteen, managed to overcome that hurdle, fills me with self pride. I really hope you have enjoyed the story of Operation Cavalry and could overlook my lack of experience. Now, I don't know if I'll ever get round to writing it but I do have a sequel planned (as was evident in the epilogue.) So look out for that.

If you enjoyed my work, have any legitimate criticisms or just want to support me, please leave an amazon review and look out for more stuff. I don't know if I'll ever manage to achieve a novel again but I'll certainly be releasing short stories when I can. Thank you for reading.

-Theodore Scothern